G R JORDAN

The Execution of Celebrity

A Kirsten Stewart Thriller #6

First edition

ISBN: 978-1-914073-89-2

This book was professionally typeset on Reedsy.
Find out more at reedsy.com

A celebrity is a person who works hard all of their life to become well known, and then wears dark glasses to avoid being recognised.

FRED ALLEN

Contents

Foreword

This novel is set around the highlands and islands of Scotland and while using the area and its people as an inspiration, the specific places and persons in this book are entirely fictitious.

Acknowledgement

To Ken, Jessica, Jean, Colin, Susan and Rosemary for your work in bringing this novel to completion, your time and effort is deeply appreciated.

Novels by G R Jordan

The Highlands and Islands Detective series (Crime)

1. Water's Edge
2. The Bothy
3. The Horror Weekend
4. The Small Ferry
5. Dead at Third Man
6. The Pirate Club
7. A Personal Agenda
8. A Just Punishment
9. The Numerous Deaths of Santa Claus
10. Our Gated Community
11. The Satchel
12. Culhwch Alpha
13. Fair Market Value
14. The Coach Bomber
15. The Culling at Singing Sands
16. Where Justice Fails
17. The Cortado Club
18. Cleared to Die
19. Man Overboard!

Kirsten Stewart Thrillers (Thriller)

1. A Shot at Democracy
2. The Hunted Child
3. The Express Wishes of Mr MacIver
4. The Nationalist Express
5. The Hunt for 'Red Anna'
6. The Execution of Celebrity
7. The Man Everyone Wanted

The Contessa Munroe Mysteries (Cozy Mystery)

1. Corpse Reviver
2. Frostbite
3. Cobra's Fang

The Patrick Smythe Series (Crime)

1. The Disappearance of Russell Hadleigh
2. The Graves of Calgary Bay
3. The Fairy Pools Gathering

Austerley & Kirkgordon Series (Fantasy)

1. Crescendo!
2. The Darkness at Dillingham
3. Dagon's Revenge
4. Ship of Doom

Supernatural and Elder Threat Assessment Agency (SETAA) Series (Fantasy)

1. Scarlett O'Meara: Beastmaster

Island Adventures Series (Cosy Fantasy Adventure)

1. Surface Tensions

Dark Wen Series (Horror Fantasy)

1. The Blasphemous Welcome
2. The Demon's Chalice

Chapter 01

Kirsten Stewart lay face down, her head turned to one side as she breathed deeply. She was unsure what time of the night it was, possibly more like early morning. Beside her sounded the snores of a man. She had one arm draped over him but had turned her head because he'd rolled his over so that the rushing air from his snoring would've been rolling straight into her face. It wasn't the romantic moment that she'd always dreamed of. Then again, she'd got used to the idea that romantic ideals were very rarely fulfilled. On the other hand, he was here.

She reached over with her arm, pulling him tighter, her hand feeling his bare side. Kirsten heard a little grunt and she gave him a squeeze. It wasn't enough to wake him, and she wasn't going to be that mean, for Kirsten was happy. The last month had been quiet in her job. She led the north of Scotland section of one of secret services within the United Kingdom. Dark government organisations, there to protect from threats that the everyday police personnel would struggle with, be it terrorism, extortion or incidents that would cause a global scandal. More recently, it had been about information and protecting her country's secrets. On the other hand, because of what she did, she now realised she was a target.

When she was an ordinary police officer, albeit operating as a detective constable, Kirsten never felt under threat from anyone, never felt that she was targeted by any of the criminal fraternity. Recently, she'd been photographed along with Craig, her lover and fellow cohort within the services, while they'd been away on a romantic rendezvous far from others' eyes. At least that's what she'd thought. The arrival of the man with a camera and then the speedy chase which led to him disappearing in a nearby wagon, had given her food for thought.

Kirsten was restless, so she grabbed the bed clothes, flung them back off her, and made her way across the dark bedroom and out to the kitchen of her house. She thought about grabbing her dressing gown, but the dark of the bedroom meant that she couldn't see it and she wasn't going to switch on the light in case she woke Craig up. Besides, who would see her?

She mooched out to the kitchen, where she switched on the light and turned on the kettle, before making her way back into the lounge and finding a jumper she'd been wearing the day before. She put it on right as the kettle clicked and then made herself a black coffee before sitting down on the sofa in the living room. Part of her thought she should switch on the television, but the silence of the night felt good. Kirsten continued to sit, closing her eyes while sipping her coffee.

Then she heard them. Footsteps coming up the stairs outside. Kirsten's flat was on the second floor. The clip clop of heels making their way up the stairs made her open her eyes and then jump off the sofa, making her way to her drawer on the far side of the room. She removed the gun from it, one of the three she had in the house, and made her way behind the sofa, crouching down and awaiting the arrival of the footsteps.

Of course, there were no guarantees that this was anyone of note to her or that they were even coming to her flat. But after the incident with the photographer, Kirsten didn't take chances.

The footsteps came closer, sounding louder in the quiet of the night before they stopped right outside her door. Kirsten stood up and quickly made her way over to beside the door, giving herself a position where if someone forced it open, she could take them out instantly. Then she waited.

In this job, you had to keep your heart from racing. There were too many moments that in normal life would give you palpitations, but she breathed deeply, controlling her pulse, eyes locked on the door. She could hear something fiddling at the lock and realised that whoever it was there, they were trying to break in quietly. Well, they would get a shock.

It took thirty seconds before she saw the door start to part gently and a face looked inside. The outside light of the stairwell, which wasn't that strong, meant that the person entering was in silhouette.

Kirsten let the person walk in. The person looked left, then right, and started to walk towards the bedroom. Quickly, Kirsten followed and put a gun to the back of the intruder's head.

'Enough. On your knees now.'

The person dropped down. Kirsten thought she recognised the hair. The height was right as well. Slowly, she dropped the gun away from the woman's neck and made her way over to the light switch.

'Can't you just knock like anyone else?' asked Kirsten.

'I didn't want to disturb you and thought it was easier doing this. I knew you were here. I take it he's up.'

'Yes, he's staying with me, but he's not up out of bed. He's lying sleeping in that room.' Kirsten watched Anna Hunt, her boss, get to her feet and turn around. She was wearing a smart black overcoat and gave Kirsten a quick smile.

'That's good to see you enjoying yourself, but you're going to have to tell him he's making breakfast on his own.'

'What? Has the First Minister been shot or something?'

'Don't be melodramatic,' said Anna, strolling over to the kitchen, switching on the kettle. 'But you need to get yourself dressed. Do you always swan around in the middle of the night with just a jumper on?'

'I can afford the heating bill, so why not?' said Kirsten, and walked over to the bedroom door. 'Just fix yourself a coffee. I'll only be a moment.'

Kirsten stepped inside the bedroom, made her way over to where Craig was sleeping and sat down beside him. She gently wrapped her arms around him, whispering in his ear.

'Anna Hunt's here. I don't know where I'm going or why I'm going, but it doesn't look like I'll be back before lunch, so have a lie-in.'

She felt a pair of hands pulling her down towards him. After a long kiss and a few moments of intimate contact, she stood up and made her way over to her wardrobe. She emerged from the bedroom in a pair of black jeans, a black t-shirt, and a leather jacket.

'Good. Ready for business,' said Anna, downing the rest of her coffee before placing the cup in the sink.

'There is a dishwasher,' said Kirsten.

'That's a quality cup,' said Anna. 'I wouldn't want to see it

4

get damaged.'

Kirsten recognised the cup was the one that she'd been given by her detective team when she left the force to join the service. It wasn't a quality cup, but it did mean something to her. At least, Anna recognised that.

Ten minutes later, they were in the car driving to the outskirts of Inverness. Kirsten could see flashing lights of police cars, as well as a small contingent of press, and they parked up a short distance away. Anna reached into the boot of her car, taking out a couple of bibs that read 'police' across the back. They both donned them and made their way up to the police cordon around the house. The women took out their IDs, showed them to the constable on duty, then walked up between the two large pillars that flanked either side of the door of the house. *Surely the place must have about eight bedrooms*, thought Kirsten. It was the biggest house that she'd seen in a long time, and certainly one that she could never afford.

'Who lived here then and why are we here?'

'DJ. You probably hear him every morning on the radio.'

'No,' said Kirsten, 'don't tend to listen to the radio. If I do, it's Radio 4.'

Anna Hunt stopped and turned. 'Radio 4? Thought it's just chitchat. Thought you'd want to get away from current affairs and anything like that.'

'I don't listen to it for what it's saying; I listen to it for the sound. It's very relaxing.'

'I thought you were brought up in a mixed martial arts ring. I thought you would have loud music—heavy metal and all that.'

'Not when I'm outside, but when I want to relax. But who

was he then, or she?'

'This is the home of Scotland's favourite DJ, Angus "Hootsman" Argyle, and he was kidnapped earlier on tonight at gunpoint in front of his family.'

Kirsten made her way into the hallway. Through an open door, she could see a woman in tears sitting on the sofa.

'That's his Missus,' said Anna, 'but we're not here to talk to her. We're going to talk to the inspector in charge.'

Kirsten stopped for a moment, looked at Anna. 'Macleod?'

'Of course it's not Macleod. He's been kidnapped, not murdered. At least not yet,' said Anna, lowering her voice, making sure that no one inside that living room could hear. 'Come on; he'll probably be at the back here.'

Anna walked through to a large kitchen at the rear of the house and Kirsten looked around, realising that the one in her flat was so meagre by comparison. She thought of hers as modern, but no, this, this was modern. Even the fridge was bigger than Kirsten.

'Inspector Trawlish, pleased to meet you.'

Kirsten looked at a tall woman reaching over six foot with short, cropped, blonde hair. The eyes turned on Kirsten and then on Anna, with her lips not moving. After a moment, the woman spoke. 'And you are?'

'The woman they told you to expect. You can call me Anna. This is Kirsten.'

'Okay. I guess if I asked for ID, it wouldn't do any good, would it, because the names wouldn't match.'

'That's correct, but you knew we were coming and we're here. What's the deal?'

'The deal is that this is my investigation. I'm in charge of this.'

'Absolutely,' said Anna. 'I'm not looking to usurp your authority. This is your case. I've been brought in to consult. To keep an overall view of things that are going on.'

'Well, the long and the short of it,' said Trawlish, 'is that tonight, four people came in wearing balaclavas and holding guns, and took Angus Argyle away in a black van. The said black van is now on the other side of Inverness, burnt out. Forensics are looking over it. Here, our attackers are ranging anything from five feet six up to six feet. We believe they're male, although we can't confirm that fully, and the woman inside there is in a complete state. Forensics have been in but there's nothing left. They used handheld guns, but the woman can't identify them and we're struggling to find out why anyone would seriously want to kidnap Angus Argyle.'

'What's your next move, Inspector?' asked Anna.

'Pretty stuck with doing the usual thing of feelers around town, see if anybody knows. Forensics came up with something. We'll play that through. We're looking at CCTV across Inverness, see if we can track the van, see where it came from beforehand, but to be honest, we are struggling for now though we have only just got going. But can you tell me, Anna,' said Trawlish, giving her a hard stare, 'just why the hell have I got two people from my country's most secret services at my crime scene? I didn't call for you.'

'No,' said Anna, 'I called myself in. One of my contacts, approximately twenty-four hours ago, was at a high-level meeting of figures. Said figures met in a place with no names and were taken there under hoods. At the meeting was distributed some literature.'

'Literature? What do you mean, literature?'

Anna turned to the table. From inside her coat pocket, she

pulled out a small A4 brochure and placed it on the table. It was styled in almost a childish effort, but the bold letters across the top said *The Execution of Celebrity*.

'My contact was at a meeting where people were funding what that brochure says.'

Kirsten leaned forward, Trawlish and she contacting shoulders as they looked down. Kirsten's eyes darted across the script in front of her. The brochure talked about the public execution of various high-profile figures. None were given by name, but they were all said to be key Scottish persons, those higher up in public life.

'When I heard that Mr. Argyle had been kidnapped, I felt this might be of use to you,' said Anna.

'Bollocks,' said Trawlish. 'You didn't know. You came here because you thought he's involved. You're giving me this in case I come up with anything to fire it towards you. This is crazy. Is it genuine?'

'Very,' said Anna, 'but I suggest you keep it to yourself, or at least the top level of your team. By all means, get your forensic people to have a look over it.'

Kirsten spotted there was blood at the top of the brochure.

'Was it a struggle getting it?' asked Kirsten.

'I'll get forensics onto that,' said Trawlish. 'Sheila can come up with someone.'

'You won't, or if you do, they will find nothing. That's the blood of my agent.'

'Okay,' said Trawlish. 'Have it your way. Do you have a contact number?'

Anna took a card from inside her pocket and handed it over. 'Ring that, you'll get me.' Trawlish reached inside her jacket to hand a card over to Anna.

8

'I have your number. It's not a problem,' said Anna. 'If I need you, I'll be in touch. Good luck, Inspector.'

Anna turned, causing Kirsten to feel slightly disoriented before catching up with her in the hallway and leaving the house.

'Is that it?' asked Kirsten. 'We're not even going to go and talk to people?'

'We didn't come here to bolster their investigation,' said Anna. 'We came here to give that information to Trawlish, for you to see the scene. Reports from all the forensic people, from Trawlish, from all our team, you'll get access to. That won't be a problem.'

'The brochure though, you said it's genuine.'

'It is.' Kirsten noticed that Anna swallowed hard at that point.

'And the blood, that's genuine too,' said Kirsten. 'But you said to Trawlish to just keep quiet on identifying who it was. Then that means—'

'Yes,' said Anna. 'She's dead. It's one of my Glasgow operatives, and she's dead. Died getting this to me.'

As they got into the car, Anna turned and looked at Kirsten. 'I want these people. They took one of our own. I'm too close. I need someone to run this for me. Besides, my prancing about gets noticed, especially coming down into this level. You understand how the police services work—you were one. You were a constable, a detective constable, and you've got contacts. Find these people. Save these celebrities, and when you find whoever took out my agent, put a bullet in them for me.'

Chapter 02

Kirsten stepped out of Anna Hunt's car and leaning back in, shook her boss by the hand. The morning was starting to flood the sky, blue and cold, and Kirsten was shaking the blurriness from her own eyes. Craig and she had been up late the night before and then Anna had woken, or rather, Anna had interrupted her night walking. Kirsten wondered if Craig was still in her flat, maybe waiting for an update to see if he should hang around or whether he should get back to his own work if she was going to be busy.

'Just remember what I said to you,' Anna commented as she started the engine. 'There's a Danny Lowman that my contact was talking to. He's up this part of the world. Probably best to get on to him, see what he knows, but my contact was also investigating New World Order.'

'Didn't you get any updates?'

'No,' said Anna. 'I got an emergency panic button and by the time we got to it, she was already dead, but the brochure was tucked away, hidden on her. It was wrapped up in an envelope. It just said "Anna".'

'Well, I'm sorry. It seems like you're taking this quite hard.'

Anna Hunt turned around, stared at Kirsten. 'I take every

loss hard. These are my people, like you are, like Dom is, Carrie-Anne and Justin. I'd take a loss of any of you hard and if somebody comes for my people and kills them, I'll come back at them. They'll know not to do it twice.'

Kirsten shut the door and Anna drove off up the street, leaving Kirsten standing outside her office building. The downstairs of the building was just opening, a retail shop that provided cover for the work that went on upstairs. The current occupier downstairs, Gladys, was sprucing up the shop and bid Kirsten a good morning. Gladys was one of those unique people in that she was a doorkeeper, but she got to keep whatever money the business was taking, all rent-free as well.

Kirsten climbed up the stairs. By the time she reached the top, she could see Carrie-Anne at the far end of the landing. The woman was remarkable as ever, dressed in a snappy black suit. The only thing that was giving way was the lack of stilettos, forgone for a comfy pair of elegant boots.

'We're ready for you when you are, boss,' said Carrie-Anne. Kirsten shouted over to the conference room, 'In five.' Entering her office, Kirsten noted that the light was on. When she stepped inside, she saw Craig dressed in a pair of jogging bottoms and a jumper that he'd been wearing around the flat when they were having a lazy day.

'What are you doing here?' she asked.

'Well, I thought I should come and see you. It's just once you left, there was someone knocking around your flat. I was looking out the window, and saw them going up and down. I thought it was a bit odd, so I continued to watch them. Then I made a move down the stairs, watching them from inside the building. When I came out, I approached them but they made

11

off in a car.'

'Did you get the registration plate?' asked Kirsten.

'I already gave it to Justin, it doesn't exist and it was a blue Vauxhall Corsa, so hey, plenty of them about.'

'Are you okay?' asked Kirsten, thinking that Craig looked a bit spooked.

'Not overly, but why? Why are they looking at us? Why are they looking at your flat?'

'You know for sure it was me?'

'Really, who else lives in that block of flats that you know would have photographs taken of them? It wasn't a local PI trying to see if the husband's up to no good. These guys were cautious, got out of the way quickly when anyone approached, and they're running around with a false number plate. Not a stolen number plate, not a copied number plate, but a different one. One that doesn't exist. Something's up here.'

'What did the man look like?'

'Five-foot eleven, black hair, didn't get a look at his face, had a hat on as well. Dark grey trench coat. Looked like he could be a press photographer, but he wasn't. They don't go around in cars like that.'

'No,' said Kirsten, 'they don't. After the last time, I think we better be careful.'

'I'm always careful and you did a good job of sneaking away.'

'Couldn't help it. Anna's got a problem. She came all the way up to Inverness to go and view a crime scene with me.'

'Should I ask what it is?'

'It's a bit strange, to be honest. Some celebrities could be in trouble. Anna's lost one of our own over it. She wasn't in a good mood.'

'Well, understandable.'

12

Kirsten made her way across the room, wrapped herself around Craig and planted a kiss onto his lips. He accepted and together they embraced for a few moments before Kirsten stepped back. 'I've got to go and brief the team. You're welcome to stay at the flat, but I probably won't be about for a while. Could be in here working this one.'

'I'll get back then and get out. I'm meant to be down in London anyway tomorrow. You take very good care.'

'I will,' said Kirsten. She watched Craig walk across the room, open the door, step out and then step back in again.

'Oh, another thing,' said Craig. 'If you want, you can put something on when you go to get a coffee in the kitchen in the middle of the night. I'm just saying.'

'You were watching, and you didn't say,' said Kirsten.

'Oh, there was no way I was saying, trust me, but for future reference.' Craig shut the door as a block of paper was thrown towards him. Kirsten watched it crash and started to giggle to herself. That was the thing about Craig; he knew how to get under her skin, how to wind her up just enough, so that it was funny.

She pulled her coat off and hung it up, stepped across the room and picked up the block of paper before putting it down beside her printer. She took a couple of deep breaths, stepped across to the window, and looked down at the street below. There was no one there taking photographs, but then again, this was a harder street to do that on. Gladys would be out to them. She would have a quiet word, move people on, or if she thought they were really trouble, pull them in. She was the most brutal florist Kirsten had ever seen.

Having composed herself, Kirsten made her way into the briefing room and saw at the table Justin, the man who ran the computer side of business, Dom, the field operative, and Carrie-Anne, the analyst and also part-time field operative. The blonde woman nodded towards Kirsten, indicating with it the question of whether Kirsten wanted coffee. It was a vigorous nod and Carrie-Anne turned back and poured the filtered coffee into a cup before placing in on the table at Kirsten's seat. Dom was already drinking one, but he put it down and studied his boss's face meticulously.

'This is not good,' said Dom. 'What's up?'

'I was disturbed in the early hours of the morning by Anna Hunt. Came up all the way from Glasgow to speak to me. We took a trip out to the far side of Inverness, out where the proper posh houses are. Some of you may have seen the news this morning. A local DJ, Angus Argyle, was kidnapped at gunpoint in front of his family.'

'I saw that,' said Dom. 'What's that got to do with us? It's a DJ.'

'What's that got to do with us is this.' Kirsten put her phone down. After pressing a few buttons on her screen, an image of the leaflet was displayed up on a screen on the wall.

'What's that?' asked Dom.

'It's a kind of brochure. It's not that well made, but basically, it's describing the execution of various public figures.'

'So what, somebody's actually warned us? Is he part of it?'

'No, Dom,' said Kirsten. 'We don't know. It's very general what's said in the brochure, but it's a description of how lots of public figures are going to be hung for the way in which society has been treated by them. People sponging. People deluding the public from a meaningful life. Lots of gobbledygook and jabbering like that.'

'Where did the brochure come from?' asked Carrie-Anne.

'It was on a dead agent, one of Anna Hunt's. She activated an emergency beacon while investigating a certain activist. When Anna Hunt got to her, the woman was dead, but this brochure was hidden away inside her clothes in an envelope with Anna's name on it. Lo and behold, not long after, Angus Argyle was taken under gunpoint. What we know of the grab, it was done by a well-trained bunch of people. I doubt forensics is going to get much, but I have been in touch with Inspector Trawlish, and we'll be getting whatever she gets.'

'This for real?' asked Dom. 'We really think that celebrities are going to be grabbed and then hanged somewhere? How are they going to do that? Are they going to stage it? What's the point behind it?'

'The point behind it, Dom, is we don't know what terrorist group is behind it. Look at the brochure. It just talks about the rights and wrongs of these sponges of society. It doesn't actually go into a lot of depth, so we don't know where it's coming from. It doesn't have any logo attached to it, any activist group that we are aware of. Anna said in the previous conversations with her contact, she was talking about a Danny Lowman.'

'Danny Lowman?' muttered Justin Shivers, chirping in for the first time in the conversation.

'You know him?' asked Kirsten.

'Know of him. Activist, support group seeking to overthrow the current world order. Bit of a nut job. Could find him easy enough.'

'Good,' said Kirsten. 'Dom and Carrie-Anne, if Justin finds him, you're going to speak to him.'

'She also heard about a new other group called—'

'New World Order,' said Justin.

'Why? She tell you that?' asked Kirsten.

'Hot topic at the moment. I'll dig more into it, but I do remember Danny Lowman, his connections to New World Order, or rather, he voiced support for them. I'm not sure he's tied into it himself. Dom and Carrie-Anne can find out when I find him.'

'Is there anything else to go on?' asked Carrie-Anne. 'Any other leads?'

'No,' said Kirsten. 'We're not even sure where Anna's contact was, why she got discovered and killed, but I can tell you this, Anna's seriously pissed. She told me in the car that when we find these people, just to take them out.'

'She's fiercely loyal if nothing else,' said Dom. 'What's the thing with Craig coming in this morning? I thought he was staying at your place anyway. I got here and Gladys is holding him downstairs. Wouldn't let him upstairs until I got here.'

'Good. At least, she knows her business,' said Kirsten. 'Craig was at mine last night. He said after I left, in the early hours of the morning, somebody was downstairs on the street with a camera, taking photographs like the incident we had before.'

'What, the one where the guy turned up trying to photograph you when you were both on retreat away in the Cairngorms?'

'That one,' said Kirsten. 'I don't understand why people are coming and taking photographs all the time.'

'Craig all right on his own?' asked Dom.

'He's fine. They're just taking photographs now. He knows how to stay good. Anyway, that's what I've got for you. I'm going to oversee what comes from Inspector Trawlish. I'm trying to pull together any other evidence that there is. Anna's going to send me up a file on her agent. I'll go through that as well. Justin, get the address for Danny Lowman. Dom and Carrie-Anne, when he gets that, get after Lowman, shake him down. I need to know what's going on. We've got one kidnapped celebrity. From this brochure, we may get a lot more. Best we nip it in the bud before it actually happens.'

'Does it give any indication of which celebrities? Any indication of names? Because to be honest, boss, I wouldn't have picked Angus Argyle as a particularly big target. Has he said anything recently?'

'He doesn't say anything,' said Carrie-Anne. 'He's on the show in the morning. Two hours of benign pop and all that stuff. Win prizes, blah, blah, blah. He's nobody in one sense but guess he's everybody in the celeb world.'

'Maybe that could be it,' said Kirsten. 'Maybe that's the point. I don't know but keep an open mind on it. Get out there and find Danny Lowman. Justin, get me everything on the New World Order you can. All right then, briefing over. Let's get to work.'

Chapter 03

Dom hung on the shoulder of Justin Shivers as he typed into the computer. Watching the screen, each data entry flashing by, he wondered how on earth Justin was even checking any of them. The man would occasionally type in other information, none of which Dom was privy to, but it struck him that Justin was getting slightly frustrated.

'He's good, I'll give him that. He's jumping around. There's no fixed abode coming up. I've linked him back through his pages. Three different websites, even going back into the dark web, but so far, no addresses. Well, at least nothing but web addresses. If I could just get something that ties him into the system.'

Dom turned away, looked at Carrie-Anne, the two of them feeling decidedly useless. The blonde woman stepped up, crouched down beside Justin, and looked at the screen.

'It doesn't actually make any difference whether you're on my shoulder, at my side, or whether you're staring at the screen. The computer does what it does. I do what I do, and the answer will come out when the answer comes out. You might as well go and sit and get a coffee somewhere.'

'It doesn't look good, though, does it,' said Dom. 'The boss comes in and there's the two of us sat with our feet around the coffee, and then as soon as you say something, we try and blame it on you.'

'Fine. Go and stand in the corner and stare at the wall.'

Dom could tell that Justin was getting annoyed. Clearly, things were proving harder than he thought they would be. Carrie-Anne walked over to Dom, tapped him on the shoulder, and indicated they should go to the far end of the room. Once there, she put an image of the brochure up on the screen and began staring at it.

'Kirsten lifted all the information from that,' said Dom. 'You might as well stare at his screen up there than stare at this one.'

'Maybe, but it just helps me think,' said Carrie-Anne, and gave Dom a grimace. Clearly, he wasn't keen to alleviate Justin's annoyance.

'That's you,' said Justin, suddenly. 'There we go. Okay, we've now got a driving license. He's put it down as Danny Laumann, in the German. He is a shifty guy. Right, here's your address,' said Justin, writing something down on a piece of paper and holding it out. Carrie-Anne stood over, picked it up, and took a look.

'Oh, the rough end,' she said. 'All right, let's go get Dom out to flex his muscles there before he goes daft in this building.' Justin laughed. Carrie-Anne could see the man wind down somewhat.

'Of course, we might be back,' said Carrie-Anne, 'if this is a dud.'

'Don't you dare,' said Justin, giving the woman a stare.

Carrie-Anne let Dom drive to the other side of Inverness. They turned into what was a rather rough-looking estate, with

19

some boarded-up houses, windows with wood across them, and one looked as if it had a fire in it quite recently, with scorch marks on the outside. Two doors down from that one was the house allegedly owned by Danny Laumann. He also seemed not to pay council tax because of the difficulty he had with benefits.

'How do you want to play it?' asked Carrie-Anne. 'You just going to burst in? Are you going to be one of the inspectors?'

'Council Inspector,' said Dom. 'Let's talk about his council tax. If he's much of extremist, he'll want to rant at me.'

They got out of the car and Carrie-Anne watched Dom adjust his tie before stepping across and fixing it for him. He could never do it quite right. It always sat to the side, and she felt that she couldn't leave him like that, the image of a slightly distressed official.

Dom walked down the short drive and looked at the shopping trolley that was sitting in the unmown lawn to the front of the house. He looked for a bell to press, but there was none, and so, instead, thundered the door with his fist.

Carrie-Anne slid round to the side of the house, checking to see where the rear door was, if there was any escape out the back, but returned quickly. The door opened and a man in jogging bottoms with a rather stained t-shirt looked at them. His hair was unkempt, and his bushy eyebrows gave him the appearance of an owl.

'Excuse me, I'm looking for Danny Laumann,' said Dom.

'Aye,' said the man. 'Who wants to know?'

'I'm from the Council. It appears you have council tax arrears. Quite substantial ones as well.'

'I don't pay council tax,' said the man, 'on account of my benefits.'

'It's not what I've got here,' said Dom. In front of him, he held a clipboard. There was nothing written on the paper on the clipboard, but Danny couldn't see that. Dom just kept shaking his head. 'I'm afraid we're going to have to start some proceedings. Get the bailiffs out.'

'You don't need bailiffs. I told you, I don't owe anything. I'm on benefits.'

Dom cast a glance at the man and then looked beyond him. 'You're right,' said Dom. 'We don't have to get the bailiffs. I've brought one with me,' and turned to Carrie-Anne. 'Let me introduce Miss Heidi Stone. She's a debt collector, and she's authorised to come in and take any item within your house that she deems worthwhile, to the value that you owe us.'

'No, she isn't. You can't just do that. I'll call the police.'

'Fine, they can restrain you,' said Dom, 'if you get in our way. It's all above board and legal. It says right here.' Dom tapped the piece of paper. The man stepped forward and Carrie-Anne slid past them into the house.

'Oi,' said the man. 'What are you doing?'

'Looking for some suitable items,' said Carrie-Anne. She opened the door to her left and inside she found the room was quite hot. There were several green plants sitting around.

'Is this how you make your money?' asked Carrie-Anne, striding across the room. She ignored the plants and walked to a room at the rear. When she opened it up, she saw the room was dark except for several screens and she heard the whir of a large number of computers.

'That server over there, that will do for starters,' said Carrie-Anne.

There was a scream from the man behind. 'No, it won't,' he said. 'You can't take any of this stuff. This is mine.'

21

Dom had arrived behind him. 'Are you a gamer then?' said Dom. 'How are you able to afford all this stuff?'

'It's all legit,' said the man.

'Really?' said Carrie-Anne. 'I'm not sure if I can take this one. We may want to get the police. I think that's counterfeit.'

'Leave it alone. Out, I tell you, you have no right coming in here.'

Carrie-Anne strode over to one of the screens in the far corner. She saw the words *The New World Order* with violent images below it. On another screen, there was a webchat running and she was able to cast her eye across it, seeing what she could certainly define as hate speech among the comments. She turned to Dom and nodded. He turned on his heel, walked out to the front door, and made sure it was shut before returning.

'Look, love,' said Danny to Carrie-Anne. 'I think we got off on the wrong foot here. How about I just give you some money to pay this off?'

Carrie-Anne put her arm out, placed a hand on the man's shoulder, and pushed him down into one of his computer chairs. 'How about you sit down and tell us a few things.'

'What do you mean?' he asked. 'What's all this about?'

Dom sat down beside the man. 'You see the thing is I'm not from the council and she's not from the debt collectors either. It's much worse than that, seeing the stuff on the screen here.'

'Hey, I haven't let any details out. Nobody knows, I'm good. I'm good. Any of the stuff that goes up on the web, all the promotional things, you can tell them, it's not a problem. Nobody's going to catch anything off it. Nobody's coming after you through here.'

'The thing is,' said Dom, 'We're not from them either. We

22

want to know what's going on. Angus Argyle just got taken away at gunpoint. A little bird told me you might know something about that. Something about an event coming up.'

'That,' he said, looking at them. 'Okay, I take it you're from the police.' Don nodded, not wanting to let on who he really was. 'Just let me go over here a minute. I get you all the stuff on it.' Carrie looked at Dom, but he nodded, indicating the man should be left to rise.

Danny Lowman made his way across the room, which was still dark, except for the bright screens. Carrie-Anne tried to see what the man was doing as he reached inside a drawer, but she couldn't see clearly until the man spun around. By the time he had fired, Dom had thrown himself to the floor and Carrie-Anne had stepped to one side. The shot hit the far wall, making a hole through it. The weapon wasn't silenced, and Carrie-Anne reckoned that the sound would be heard well outside.

Before Danny could fire another shot, Carrie-Anne had moved back into his line of sight, put her hand up to his wrist, and driven an elbow into the man's stomach. Yet, he fired again, causing Carrie-Anne to throw herself to one side. However, she still had a hand on his wrist, twisting it, and the gun fell, but she had to take herself to the ground to get out of the line of fire.

'Bloody hell,' the man shouted. 'That's my wrist.' As he tore off out of the room, Dom tried to reach back and grab his leg, but missed him, causing Carrie-Anne and he to scurry back to their feet.

'You need to get him before he goes outside, Dom,' she said.

'I know,' came a terse reply. As they tore past the plants, several had been knocked over. Dom exited the living room

23

to find Danny just opening the door and about to step outside. He reached for him, but the man turned and caught Dom in the face with the back of his hand. Following up behind, Carrie-Anne dipped her shoulder, and the three of them crashed out through the open door, onto the drive below. As the man lay writhing on the ground, Dom rolled over, got on top of him, and slapped some cuffs on him.

'You're small fry,' said Dom, 'don't do this. Don't protect them or you'll go down for it. They'll lock you up.'

'For what?'

'You're saying I won't come up with anything when we scour through all that hardware inside? You know something's up. Public executions.'

Dom could see the man turn away. 'Tell me.' Dom drove the man's arm up behind his back.

'Arghh,' said the man, 'bloody hell.'

'I'll do it again,' said Dom. 'Tell me, what do you know?' He could see tears in the man's eyes.

'All I know is something big's going down, but I don't know what. You don't get told something like that.'

'You didn't hear it. The dark web or your chatrooms?' asked Dom.

'No, nothing. It's just something big.'

'Dom,' said Carrie-Anne, 'Who's that bloke over there?' Dom looked up. There was a man standing in what looked like a press jacket. He was holding a camera, pointing it in their direction. Before Dom could answer the question, Carrie-Anne was off and she ran through the garden, put one foot on the upturned trolley, and jumped the wall into the street. Outside, the man with the camera saw her coming and turned to flee, but Carrie-Anne was quick.

As the man raced along the street, his camera in one hand, Carrie-Anne began to catch up with him as he approached the car. A door was flung open. Carrie-Anne realised that he would reach the car before she got to him. She drove her legs harder and then dived, flinging herself forward. With her right hand she stretched, clipping the man's back heel causing that foot to go inside its current path. His two feet collided and he went headfirst into the side of the car.

'Get in,' yelled a man from inside. 'You two, get him in!'

A pair of hands came out, grabbing the man, but Carrie-Anne had now rolled to her feet. As he was grabbed towards the car, she reached out and managed to put a hand onto the strap of the camera. The man was being dragged to the car with the camera strap choking him as Carrie-Anne held fast to it.

'We got to go. We got to go,' shouted the man in the front.

'The bitch has got the camera. She's got a hold of the camera.'

'Just let it go,' said the man, 'just let it go.'

With that, somebody cut the strap, and Carrie-Anne fell backward, the camera strap in her hands. There was a crash as the camera hit the street, and the car began to drive away. It swerved this way and that before the door managed to close, but not before it hit the man being dragged inside on the head. Carrie-Anne tried to adjust herself, get back to her feet, and tried to remember the number plate that had just disappeared.

More than likely untraceable, she thought, *going to be either that, or it will be stolen.* She walked back to the house of Danny Lowman. She could see the neighbours who had begun to arrive, poking their noses out from their doors.

'He told you anymore?' she asked.

'No,' Dom said, 'I don't think he knows anything more.'

25

'He's broke my arm,' said the man. 'I swear he broke my arm.'

Dom began to uncuff him, turned to Carrie-Anne, and shook his head. 'Nothing else coming from here. This guy's small fry.'

'Hey, I am small fry. I'm just the publicity. Bastards like you that have us the way we are.' The man was still lying on his front, arms behind his back. Dom gave him a kick before he left.

'I really don't like people like that,' he said to Carrie-Anne. 'I guess he was probably an early contact. Probably been closed off by anyone about to carry this out. They're not going to be speaking to anyone like him.'

'Remember to get somebody to pay him a visit, later on,' said Carrie-Anne. 'Get a line on those computers. I'll see if Justin can deal with that now he's got a physical position to do it from.' The pair got into the car and Dom drove off with Carrie-Anne holding the camera in front of her.

'What's on it?' he asked.

'Screen's broke, smashed when I fell. Guess we're going to be working overtime on this one.'

Chapter 04

Kirsten was sitting in her office when there was a knock on the door; she flicked her head around to see who it was. A smile came across her face, for Craig was looking in. He opened the door almost apologetically.

'What are you doing here? You 're meant to be getting a flight.'

'Anna Hunt called, just wanted me to pick something up from Justin. Then I'll be getting on my way. Where is he?'

'He's just through in his office.' said Kirsten, 'but come here a minute.'

Craig padded into the room, wondering what was coming. Kirsten stood up, flung her arms around him, and held on tight for a few moments. 'You're not getting away without getting one of those,' she said, almost laughing. 'Your face. You think I was about to do something nasty to you?'

She felt his arm squeeze back. 'Well, you never know with you, do you?'

'Go see Justin. I've got to go to him in a minute anyway.'

'Okay,' said Craig, 'you can go first if you want. I've got myself a sandwich and I'm going to sit in here and eat it, if that's all right with you.'

'Of course, it is. Tell you what, you go see Justin; I'll follow you in afterwards. Then you can come back here, eat your sandwich, but you wait here before I come back. Sometimes you need to say goodbye properly.'

'Thought we did that?'

'Yes. Doesn't mean you don't have to get some practice in.'

She watched him walk out the door and sat back down in her chair, screening the details of various activists on the team's watch list. For the moment, Kirsten's eyes were not looking at them. Instead, she was thinking about Craig, the fact he had to keep returning to London. If she kept up this life, would her time with Craig simply be every other weekend when they could manage? In truth, she loved the work. She loved where she was, what she was doing for her country. Sure, it was dangerous, but that side didn't bother Kirsten. Yet, inside, she felt something else, something that said maybe Craig should be here permanently. Maybe she would like a permanent life with him, some place where they didn't have to disappear off and keep secrets from each other simply because of their employers.

It was five minutes later when Craig walked back into the room.

'That was a bit more than picking something up,' said Kirsten.

'That was four and a half minutes of Justin taking the rip out of me. Then thirty seconds of here's what I'll give her. Oh, and by the way, tell her this, tell her that.'

'Okay,' said Kirsten, 'I believe you. You sit there and eat your sandwich. I'll be back in a bit.' She marched off through into Justin's office to see the man as ever sitting behind his computer.

'What have we got, Justin?'

'Well, there's a lot of activity on now with that New World Order group. The thing that's getting me is there's a lot circulating on the web forums. Also, some of the dark web, certain chattering is there, but I'm coming up with nothing concrete. Just speculation. Usually, I get some idea of times, you might get something dropped in, or that this is going to happen in a certain part of the country. I've got nothing against any specific celebs or any talk of what's coming, other than something big is going to happen. I think they might have done this quite high up. This might be quite a project that's in the influencers, those at the top ranks, not something that the low levels know a lot about.'

'When they say something's coming, how do they end up knowing that then?'

'For the lower ranks, I think it's just the activity that we're seeing, but some of these activist groups, they're not capable of this. When you said that Angus Argyle was kidnapped at gunpoint in front of his family, when you talked about it, it sounded almost professional. Very slick. Not a bunch of amateurs jumping in. The number plate, made up, not just stolen.'

'That's my read on it, too,' said Kirsten. 'Currently hoping that Danny Lowman is going to come back with something. At the moment we seem very in the dark about everything. I've just come off the phone with Inspector Trawlish. I've gone over her forensic work and everything. Nothing seems amiss. They didn't find out anything, either. She's as much in the dark as when I first turned up with Anna. I don't think she has taken too kindly with our being involved. Now she's asking me for things, and it seems that our help might be wanted.'

'Well, I can sit and look through this. I'll try and trace where that brochure came from. See if it was printed on any public printers, like a shop, but in truth, it was probably done at home. That's what it looks like. I'll get in touch with Trawlish's people though, but I guess that's what the forensics are going to say.'

'Don't bother yourself. That is what they're saying.'

'Well, I'm running out of options here, boss.'

Kirsten heard a phone ringing in her office. 'Is there anything else you've got for me?' she asked Justin. The man shook his head. 'Right. Well, I've got to go take this call. In the meantime, keep on it to see if anybody mentions anything. You're right, it does seem too slick. In fact, start looking at mercenaries, any mercenaries in the area recently. Anybody been tagged.'

'Mercenaries? Why?'

'Slick job. Maybe they're activists, but maybe they're using their money to bring in people who know how to deal in the nefarious side of life.'

'Will do,' said Justin.

Kirsten turned on her heel, marched back out of the door and into her office, giving a quick smile to Craig as she picked up the phone that was still ringing.

'This is Kirsten,' she said, recognising the number calling her.

'This is Dom. Danny Lowman hasn't added up to much. He says there's something going on, but he has no idea what it is.'

'That sounds about right. Justin says the low-lives are all talking, but they're not saying anything of substance. They just know something's going to happen. I don't think any of them know anything about the brochure.'

'There is one other thing though, boss,' said Dom, 'they came to take photographs of us. We chased them down and managed to get a smashed camera, but we couldn't catch them. They disappeared off. You said you were photographed twice. Now they are photographing Carrie-Anne and me. This doesn't bode well.'

'No, it doesn't,' said Kirsten. 'Seems to me that we're being profiled. Set up for something, maybe some sort of a hit.'

'I'll be careful,' said Dom. 'I certainly think we should think about going dark.'

'Good thought, and Craig's off down the road anyway.'

'You can go to the HQ and spend some time in there.'

'We still have a job to do. Craig's heading over to the plane soon. Other than that, we operate in pairs. No one out on their own, Dom. Understood?'

'Understood. I think Carrie-Anne will warmly welcome that idea.'

'Good. I'll pass it on to Anna Hunt. She was going to do some checking anyway, see if anything was coming down the line.'

Kirsten put down the phone and caught Craig's worried face. 'Something up?' he asked.

'Yes, people have been taking photographs of Dom and Carrie-Anne now, similar to when they took photographs of us. You were photographed outside my flat. I just want to know why; why are people doing this? There could be a possible hit involved. You may be being profiled for one.'

'But why, you got anybody after you?' asked Craig.

'Not that I'm aware of. The loose ends were tied up. There's no one I can think of coming for me.'

'It could be back from your police days?'

'No,' said Kirsten, shaking her head, 'it's not. The people we dealt with then, this isn't their style.' She walked over to the window and scanned the street below but saw no one unusual and certainly no one with a camera.

'Well, I've got to go,' said Craig, 'sorry.' He stood up and Kirsten walked quickly over to him, wrapping herself around him and kissing him as passionately as possible for a brief moment.

'Take care,' she said, 'I don't like this. I don't like what's going on.'

'I'll be fine. I can handle myself. I've done this before,' said Craig.

'I'll walk you down.'

'You don't have to,' said Craig, 'really.'

'But I want to. They all know now; we don't have to be so secretive. Besides, it looks more normal, you coming up to my office where I work, me coming down to send you off from the car. People think this is a financial hub up here in these offices. Of course, we're going to escape out of the office any chance we get.'

'Okay,' said Craig. They broke off and Craig put his waste in Kirsten's bin before grabbing his jacket and opening the door. Kirsten was behind him, still dressed in her black jeans and t-shirt. She flung on her leather jacket and followed him down out through the front door shop to the street outside. Craig made his way to a car and then stopped.

'You look rattled,' he said. 'You really do.'

'I'm not rattled,' said Kirsten. 'I'm chewing things over. It's not right. It really isn't right.'

'Fine,' said Craig. 'Would you be careful, too. You said in twos when you were on the phone to Dom. Make sure you're riding two as well. Just because you're the boss doesn't mean you get to play fast and loose with the rules.'

'Of course not.' Her hands reached out to his and she held him, looking up into his eyes. 'You ever think about making this more than a weekend rendezvous?'

'Whoa,' said Craig. 'That's a big question when I'm leaving.'

'Well, it's a big feeling I've got at the moment.'

'When you say weekend rendezvous, do you mean like proper settling down or just living in the same area?'

'I don't know,' said Kirsten, and the man lifted up his hand and placed it on her cheek before letting his fingers fan out and run through her hair. 'I could do it for you,' he said. 'I could move up here.'

'Or me move down.'

'You're doing too well. You've got the section and everything.'

'I could drop that. Maybe even go for a normal life. Go back to the police. You'd see more of me then.'

'You told me that Macleod hauled you in all the time.'

'Well, yes, I thought he was a taskmaster until I met Anna Hunt. But seriously, Craig,' Kirsten squeezed his hand, 'think about it for me. Will you? Because it's playing on my mind.'

'Of course.' He reached forward to kiss her on the cheek and Kirsten felt a glow inside, but then her eyes saw something that turned her cold. There was a car approaching at speed. The street the office was located in was not wide. It could just about accommodate at two cars abreast, but this one was hurtling along at a speed that defied all sense if there was a normal driver inside. Kirsten saw the window being rolled down at the back.

'Down!' she shouted to Craig, throwing an arm around his shoulders and pulling him down with her to the ground below.

She heard glass breaking, windows shattering, blown out, but she rolled in behind a parked car wheel. Reaching inside her jacket, she pulled out her gun and saw Craig was doing the same, but the engine of the car hadn't decreased its noise. The car continued to drive along the street and as she peered up over the glass-covered bonnet of Craig's car, she could see it disappearing around the corner.

Kirsten picked up her mobile phone, punched in a code to headquarters, and started calling down the line. The car description was poor. She hadn't clocked a number plate. Who knew if they could get anywhere with tracing it? She didn't want the police racing after it either, just observing it, seeing if they could track down where it was going.

In some ways it was professional, spying them out, realising where they worked, and then going for them. Maybe they'd been tailing Craig to the airport and doubled back when he parked up and come back to the office. Or had they been waiting for an opportunity for her to come down? These questions ran through Kirsten's head as she stood up in the street, staring down at the corner the car had gone around less than a minute ago.

She felt a pair of arms wrap around her, a quiet kiss on her neck. 'We best get inside,' said Craig. 'We can't track it. We can't run after it. Let others do that. We need to get inside.'

Kirsten could feel him shaking and she let her hand slip down onto his arm and then find his hand before taking him inside. As she walked through the door, she looked at the long bay window and the shop down below where she could see an old woman looking out with a gun behind her back.

Semi-professional, thought Kirsten. *Must be semi-professional, and they don't realise this is the base. This is not somewhere to attack. If they had stopped, people would've come out of the shop and taken them out, or maybe they did realise that. Maybe it was a statement.*

Thoughts were racing through Kirsten's head, but she continued to climb the stairs inside to her office where Justin Chivers was inside.

'Are you okay?'

Kirsten nodded but saw Justin's worried face. He wasn't looking at her. He was looking at Craig.

'I'm okay,' said Craig. 'I will be.'

'Have you ever been attacked before?' asked Kirsten.

'Not like that,' said Craig. 'I don't get out much in the field, instead, chauffeuring people around or watching people. I don't get shot at.'

'Welcome to the club,' said Kirsten, and then she leaned into him. 'You ready for a quieter life?' The only reply was his arms wrapping around her again.

Chapter 05

At ten o'clock that night, Kirsten was still sitting in her office, but opposite her now was Inspector Trawlish. At first, the police thought it was a botched attempt at grabbing another celebrity, but when they realised that had been an attempted hit on one of the secret services, Trawlish had made her way there.

The woman was standing behind her chair, her arms holding onto the edge almost as if she would fall over if she didn't hang tight. Kirsten was lying back in her own chair, still dressed in the jeans and black t-shirt she'd worn that morning.

'Did you poke the bear?' asked Trawlish.

'Not that I'm aware.' said Kirsten. 'I have no evidence that this is anything to do with the case that you're on. I have no evidence that we stirred anything up. We've had people observing us for a while now.'

'That all sounds awfully unsafe,' said Trawlish. 'Maybe we should split this investigation. Let me just run with it.'

'No. I think Anna Hunt will back me up on that one.'

'Likes to be in charge, does she?'

'No,' said Kirsten. 'It's not because of the threat coming from these people. It's because the activists that are doing the kidnapping, we think may be operating at a much higher level, somewhere that you might find it awkward to reach people. It may need to be shut down in a fashion that you are not be able to operate in.'

Trawlish turned aside for a moment. 'I'm not quite sure how to take that. You're saying we can't handle it?'

'You're not equipped to handle it in the way that we would,' said Kirsten. 'I get to act sometimes when you can't. The government gives me a freer hand, shall we say.'

'I was getting more worried about the fact that I could have my officers coming under fire,' said Trawlish; 'that's why I would want it split.'

'Trust me,' said Kirsten, 'the attack isn't from this case; this isn't from the celebrity kidnapping. This is something else.'

'Again, that's why I would like it split. My guys don't carry guns; they don't get to retaliate in that fashion. Somebody comes shooting at us, we'll have to put the head down until firearms can get there and by that time it might be too late. I'm not happy about this.'

'Yes, and I'm ecstatic,' said Kirsten, causing Trawlish to whip her head around with a glance of annoyance. 'Sorry, just a bit on edge. If we fall behind the clock a bit, we can end up dead.'

'If this is where you operate from, I guess you're going to have to move.'

'Well, probably,' said Kirsten. 'But to be honest, wherever we move to, someone knows where we operate out of, someone knows where I live, but most of those people don't come looking for you. This person is hunting us down, they came to make a cold-blooded killing in the street. Most intelligence organisations don't make that sort of play. They'd find you in a dark alley, get rid of the body, leave no traces. They left a lot of bullets out there.'

'Initial report from ballistics,' said Trawlish, 'shows that they're going to be hard to trace. I'm trying to see if we can find from where they were purchased but we're not hopeful.'

'You won't find them; you'll never find the guns they came from either.'

There was a rap at the door and the diminutive figure of Anna Hunt came in. Kirsten always thought she wasn't the largest of women, but her personality could dominate a room in an instant. 'I hope my colleague has been giving you every help possible, Inspector Trawlish.'

'Close the door, please.' Trawlish waited until Anna Hunt had closed the door behind her and walked forward to stand in front of the inspector. 'Look, I know that this is your territory, and this may seem run of the mill to you, what's just happened. It's not to me and I'm worried about my people getting involved. What I don't want to do is drop off a celebrity case, because it needs investigating, but I'm not happy about putting my men and women at risk researching the same things that you are.'

'This is coming from elsewhere,' said Anna. 'Please keep your investigation going. We will try and look through other methods open to us, but we'll keep as far away from your people as possible. I agree that if they're around us at the moment, they could be brought into danger.'

Trawlish went to speak again, but a phone rang in her pocket, and she picked it out and answered the call. After she closed the call back down, she looked up at Kirsten.

'They found the car; it's burnt down on the far side. Forensics says we're going to be lucky to get anything out of it. We'll find a make and that, keep trying to discover what the numbers were, because no number plates have been found, but if I get anything else, I'll send it through to you. Just remember to send me any information you get as well.'

Trawlish marched off, agitated with the pair of women she was leaving behind. As she reached the door, Anna Hunt turned to her. 'Inspector, I understand you don't like the way we do things. I understand that you probably think we're keeping some things from you and not furnishing you with all the details. Sometimes I can't give you something because if you go investigating, you'll compromise what we're doing. You'd also be going to areas where your people could be put at risk. I hope that these celebrities are being taken by someone normal, shall we say. One of the routine criminal fraternity or a straightforward activist. However, I'm beginning to believe there may be mercenaries involved, so we will keep our involvement at this time.'

'That's understood,' said Trawlish. 'I wasted quite enough of the evening on you.' With that, she closed the door hard behind her. Kirsten could hear the woman almost tutting as she left the room.

'What a day!' said Kirsten, reaching her arms up in the air and stretching.

'Stay seated,' said Anna, 'and relax. We're going to take you through everything you've seen in the last couple of weeks. I want every detail and when I'm done with you, it's going to be Craig as well, and when I'm done with Craig, it will be Dom and Carrie-Anne. When I've got what I've got, I'll take Craig back down with me and I'm going to keep him close.'

'Close?' said Kirsten. 'You think they were targeting him?'

'No,' said Anna. 'I think they were targeting you. Craig just happened to be in the way, just happened to be that figure beside you. Yes, they may be looking to injure Craig because of you, but Craig has no enemies like this,' said Anna. 'You, you've always got the possibility of picking up enemies in this fashion.'

'How?'

'You've killed, you've stopped people achieving some big ends, you're a target. Just like I'm a target. The only thing that's gives you a semi-normal life is that most people on the other side don't choose to follow those targets. They're able to contain their anger and stay on mission, follow what they need to do for their country or organisation or whatever creed or nonsense they follow, but some people don't.'

It was after twelve when Anna had finished questioning Kirsten, and she saw Craig's worried face as he made his way into Kirsten's office to speak to Anna. An hour later Dom had to be woken up from the bunk bed in the comfort of his room where he was catching a quick sleep. And by the time Carrie-Anne had been spoken to, it was well past three in the morning. Justin arrived with pizzas and Anna indicated that Kirsten should take hers into her office where Anna would sit with her. As Kirsten fought the hot cheese that constantly burnt her mouth if she took too large a bite of it, she listened to Anna speaking, advising on the next move.

'You need to stay in this role, on this case. We need to find these kidnappers. We need to prevent any other kidnappings from happening. It's important. I've got a bad feeling in my water about this. That first kidnapping was too clean, too slick. Activists are messy. Things go wrong, people get shot, but they're messy and they're different in a really bad way. These kidnappers, yes, they may be holding him, but if we hadn't had found that brochure, you'd expect that they would just put a ransom up and send him back. I mean, he's a DJ. He's nobody.'

'He's very popular,' said Kirsten. 'I think that's the point.'

'What do you mean?' asked Anna.

'Well,' said Kirsten, 'I was thinking about this. He's banal in some ways. I mean, to you and me. I don't listen to the radio station. He's a nobody, but yet actually he gets to appear on TV at times just because of who he is. He gets to make comments. The papers even seek what he says about things that he has no clue about. Maybe that's where the anger comes from. Maybe that's what the activists wanted to do.'

'That's just a thought,' said Anna. 'You can't back any of that up.'

'No,' said Kirsten. 'What I could do is let a couple more be kidnapped and then we could tally it up. Yes, it's just a thought.'

'Don't get snappy,' said Anna. 'I know you got spooked today. Craig got really spooked. It's bothering me as well. I've already lost one down in Glasgow and now this. I couldn't tell Trawlish about the agent I lost, but that's what makes me think there's a lot more to this than just some basic activist. But for now, I want you staying on that case. Let me handle this threat. I know it's dangerous, but your team needs to be out there. Dom said you called pairs. That's a good idea when you're out in the open, but don't be afraid to work independently, either. Dom's experienced, he can handle himself. He should see it coming. Carrie-Anne is good as well. Justin, he's not as shrewd in these things. I'd probably keep him indoors. But coincidentally, he's the only one who hasn't reported seeing anybody trying to take photos of him.'

'They haven't had anybody on the street below the whole time though,' said Kirsten. 'I've been checking, watching. We'll

41

soon see it. Downstairs in the shop, they'd spot it too.'

'Don't go along those lines,' said Anna. 'Think of them as better than you. Think of them as being people who can watch you without you seeing them. Don't get sloppy. Don't think that you are the expert here. You're the prey now. You've got to think like prey. You've got to be looking for all the eyes that are coming, and just because you don't see them doesn't mean they're not there. Normally there are rules,' said Anna, standing up from her chair. 'In this spy world, there are rules. You don't take people out unnecessarily. We take them out when they have to be. There's no reason for you to be taken out. You're not testifying against anybody. You haven't got any information. No reason for Dom, Carrie-Anne to be taken out. There's no retaliation here that's on the books.'

'As far as we know.'

'What do you mean?' asked Anna.

'As far as we know. What you just said, don't think you know it. There may be retaliation here we don't know about. Like you said, I've killed people.'

Anna went quiet before reaching for a slice of pizza. She took a bite of it and chewed it, and swallowed before making any further statement and thereby allowing herself to think.

'That's a good point. I'm going to go and do some digging. In the meantime, find something to chase up on these kidnappings. I spoke to Justin earlier; he said there wasn't anything, but there's got to be. There's always a leak. There's always something. You can't just simply wait around for the next kidnapping.'

'Anna,' said Kirsten, as the woman went to leave the room.

'What?'

'Take care of Craig.'

'Okay.'

'He said agents like you, you can take care of yourselves.'

Anna walked to the door, went to open up and turned around, 'I take care of all my people. Of course, I'll take care of him.' And with that, Anna was gone from the room. Kirsten reached for the last slice of pizza, throwing it in her mouth and then regretting it as a hot chilli made her choke. She grabbed the glass of water on her desk and drank it quickly, but the burn was still there. The door opened and Craig walked in. Kirsten could still see he was shell-shocked, and she tapped her lap. The man walked over before sitting on it and wrapping his arms around her neck where he tucked in tight to Kirsten and she held him for the next minute.

There came a knock on the door. 'We've got to go. Okay?' Anna was off again.

Craig stood up but left a handout, which Kirsten took. 'Stay safe,' he said. 'Stay safe and I'll think about it for you.' After Craig had left, Kirsten watched from her window as a black car pulled up. Anna and Craig got in and then it was gone. He would fly back with Anna. He was as safe as he could be. There was a tap at the door and Carrie-Anne walked in.

'What next, boss?' she asked. 'Where do we look?'

'I don't know,' said Kirsten. 'You're the analyst. You tell me.'

Carrie-Anne said nothing but Kirsten could still feel her still standing in the room, the eyes boring into Kirsten's back. It was an off-hand comment, and it shouldn't have been made. She should have turned and helped her colleague to find the way forward, but damn it, they'd gone for Craig and she was having difficulty processing that just now.

'You tell me, Carrie-Anne; you're the damn analyst.'

43

Chapter 06

Kirstie Macintyre took the three steps up into the executive business jet and tried to smile at the stewardess looking back at her. Kirstie was the only one on the flight, making a regular trip back after a TV show in London. She never would have told anyone else, that now passing forty, she was starting to feel it. For ten years, she'd worked this show, spent most of her week down in London and then back up to her beloved Scotland. Her face was everywhere, around breakfast television, even some late afternoon shows, and every woman in the UK knew who she was. In truth, so did most of the men.

Ten years ago, newspapers spoke of her as if she was some sort of sex symbol. Then they spoke of her as a women's rights proponent, someone who was a woman of stature. Maybe that was a change of the times. Kirstie personally preferred that to the fact that she simply was now older, but she was also a realist. She moved with the times; she moved with the programme content. They got her right in the public eye, which meant that she was worth several million a year to have in front of the TV.

Her bag was taken from her, placed away in a safe locker,

and Kirstie didn't care because there was nothing she wanted to look at. It was the flight she enjoyed.

On the way down on Monday, she'd be examining what she would be doing for the week, going through the papers, combing to find out if there was any content she needed to be aware of. On Friday, she was heading home to put her feet up. Saturday, she was going to spend with her husband, at the estate they bought recently. The weather said it was going to be good and she was going to spend it in the hot tub, in the sunroom, at the rear of the mansion.

'Would you like a hot towel before we take off, Mrs Macintyre?'

'Well, thank you.' Kirstie took the warm fabric and lets its moisture spread across her face. She'd let the warmth soak deeply in past her eyes before handing the towel back.

'Ma'am, would you like a drink before we depart?'

Kirstie shook her head and looked outside at the other numerous planes on the executive apron. Time was when she had to take the regular flight down and she had to fight for every minute of airtime to get herself out there, but she'd done well. If truth be told, she believed in a lot of what she did. Yes, a lot of it was about fashion, how to look good, how to keep your face looking well, how to keep your body in shape, how to recover after having kids, and still be that woman about town. She was the one they all looked at and thought, how does she do it? *Well, in truth, you don't do it*, thought Kirstie; *you just learn to cover up and keep going. You discover how to just be.*

Kids. She always thought she was blessed with the fact she had a husband who looked after them, although the nanny helped. She should spend some time with them this weekend, although now that they were teenagers, they wanted to spend less time with her. Strange how quickly they outgrew her. All of them had complained about her being away five days a week. When they were young, they used to whine that they only ever saw her on the telly. That was the price she had paid to have made it in this world, and made it she had.

Twenty minutes passed and her jet was up at a cruising altitude much higher than she could contemplate. A glass of bubbly had arrived, and she sipped it slowly. She wondered where Jenny, the usual air hostess, was. That was a thing she'd been able to request. She flew with Mack and Gary at the front, the two pilots, then there would be Jenny and Alison. Alison was older, more her age. Sometimes Kirstie would actually sit and chat to her, but she also liked having Jenny about. She needed that younger input, just to see how she was doing.

Yes, they were polite, but she got to know them well enough that they would tell the truth, even if it was something that, maybe, Kirstie didn't want to hear. She'd been good at that, Kirstie, picking out the people to sound off properly, to get the real feel of what was happening and then adjust what she was doing based on their thoughts. Tonight, however, for some reason, the women hadn't been there.

Gary and Mack were still at the front, but the two women at the rear, she did not know. Occasionally, of course, Jenny or Alison would be off. Another attendant would come in and cover for them. Usually, it was the same couple. These two, she didn't know at all. Still, what did it matter? She wasn't needing anything and she wasn't up for talking. Kirstie sat there, drinking sparkling wine, trying to relax.

Her eyes had shut for—oh, she wasn't quite sure—but when she opened them, Kirstie was a little bit perplexed. The cabin door was sitting open, and she could see Gary's left arm. Mack was there, too, but neither of them was moving. There was no chatter from them, either. Sometimes, when the cabin door had been opened, she could hear them talking, but generally, it was shut during flight. It was due to the rules about not getting hijacked, as Kirstie remembered. She was on a private flight and there only were the three of them in the back, so they often played fast and loose with the rules.

She remembered that time standing up in the cockpit, talking to the pair of them. It was mid-cruise, not approaching the airport, and the pair were quite happy to talk to her. After all, she was paying the bills, probably a substantial part of their wages, but something didn't look right. She put her hand in the air, calling over the attendant. The woman had her hair tied up behind her and it was dark with a couple of white streaks along the side. She came over in a tartan skirt with stylish but effective black shoes.

'I'm sorry, but are they okay up there?'

'How do you mean?' asked the woman.

'Gary and Mack at the front,' said Kirstie. 'Are they okay? Sorry, what's your name, love?'

'Greta', came the reply.

'Well, Greta, they usually talk a bit more. Do you mind if I go up and see them?'

'Most pilots don't allow people up in the cockpit.'

'Well, they're used to me. They're my regular crew. They're here all the time. I'm going up to see them', said Kirstie. She didn't know why, but Greta was bothering her. After all, Kirstie was used to getting her own way.

'I'm sorry, ma'am, but you'll have to stay buckled in, possible turbulence.'

47

'What turbulence? If there's turbulence, why isn't the door shut? That door will swing here, there, and everywhere.'

'I'm sorry, ma'am, you're going to have to stay in your seat.'

'That's it', said Kirstie. She reached down, unlatched her buckle, and lifted herself out of the chair. It was a shock when Gretta swung an arm round and caught her with a punch to the chin, knocking Kirstie back into the chair.

'Sit down. Don't speak.'

Kirstie wasn't taking that. What the hell was this? She went to stand up again and saw the woman begin to swing an arm. Kirstie had done some self-defence in her time, and she managed to put her arm up in front of the swinging fist, stopping it and then delivering a punch to the woman's stomach. It had no effect, however, and the woman reached for the other hand, grabbing Kirstie's throat and shoving her down in the chair. She shouted over her shoulder, 'Ira, now.' Before Kirstie could say anything, the other hostess had arrived with silver tape, shoving it over Kirstie's mouth.

'How far have we to go?'

'Not far. Another couple of minutes. Well, we could prep her now anyway.'

Kirstie didn't know what to think, but she suddenly found herself being hauled out of the seat and thrown onto the cabin floor. Her legs were taped together, as well as her arms to her sides. She tried to struggle but there was no way to force herself out of the tape. Tears of frustration began to break in, but every time she tried to struggle, she was slapped in the face. They weren't jabs or warnings. They were brutal and blood ran from her cheek.

It felt as if the aeroplane was starting to descend, and Kirstie felt her ears beginning to go funny. The two hostesses disappeared and returned wearing black jumpsuits with parachutes tied around them. One of them seemed to have a number of extra buckles and straps. Kirstie was picked up, made to stand up while one of them stood behind her, and the other hostess connected various straps. One strap underneath Kirstie had lifted up her skirt, revealing bare thighs. *Were they going to jump, leap out with parachutes?*

The plane tilted, turning around in a circle and the hostess who was not attached to Kirstie made her way to the emergency exit. She reached down, pulled the handle, and the door was pulled away before being thrown out. Kirstie was being held up by the other hostess, her feet barely on the floor. As the woman walked along with her, Kirstie was able to glimpse to the outside of the aircraft. They were down below cloud and there was a loud rush of wind through the cabin. Her ears felt like they were bursting, and Kirstie was filled with terror.

Would they be throwing her out? How is this going to happen?

She saw one of the women walk over to her briefcase, open it up, and press some buttons inside, but then make her way over to the open door where Kirstie went out headfirst, attached to one of the hostesses.

She saw the ground from below racing up at her, until suddenly, there was an almighty jerk and she started to descend at a more comfortable rate. They had jumped out with a parachute. Looking up, Kirstie saw the large canopy above her. Below her, she saw only a beach. When she looked along the coastline, she knew she was on the east coast of Scotland. It was hard to work out exactly where she was, but as they continued to descend, she realised they were going to touch down on the beach.

The landing was not gentle. When they hit the ground, the

woman had thrown herself to the side, but Kirstie's head had been thrown down into the sand. As she was hauled back up to her feet, her head rang with pain. The second parachutist arrived shortly after and they gathered up the parachutes, before undoing the cords around Kirstie. A van pulled up, somewhere off the beach, with a number of men in masks arriving. Kirstie was lifted onto a stretcher, in a prone position, and then disappeared into the back of the van. Everything went quiet.

The tape was then pulled off her mouth and someone put their ear down close to her face, listening. There was a torchlight shone into her eyes and they seemed to check her over. Kirstie let out a scream. A vicious hand hit her hard with a slap that she was sure caused her mouth to bleed and then the tape was replaced. Kirstie's journey continued on into darkness.

* * *

The child was only five-years-old, but the wonder of a plane in the sky was something he found hard to resist. His dad was under the car bonnet working at something that the child didn't understand. And neither did the child care, for the plane had come from the right-hand-side, all the way across the sky and he'd seen two things fall from it. They were parachutes. And though they seemed quite a distance off with the plane still coming towards them, he wondered what they were doing.

Maybe it was like that Lego set he had. They were dropping food parcels. He had learned briefly about aid in his Primary 1 class. Although, quite what he understood about it, his father wasn't sure, but what next entertained the child was the fact that the plane continued for a bit and then it exploded. The child heard his father curse. The man had stood up on hearing the explosion and banged his head off the underside of the bonnet of the car.

'Jacky, what was that? Did you see what that was?'

'Aircraft up there went boom.' The child saw his dad come beside him and look up to a lot of smoke. It was then that the father took out his mobile phone and the child wondered what he was doing with it. There were games on it, but this didn't seem like a time to play games.

'Police, air traffic, something,' said the man into the phone. And the child wondered what he was doing. 'There's been an explosion. Where am I? Just north of Dundee, on the coast.' The rest of the conversation meant nothing to the child. As he stood and looked at the smoke that had billowed out from the explosion, it slowly, but surely, dissipated. And the child looked up and wondered just what had happened. When his Lego went boom, he put it all back together but he couldn't see how many of the pieces were about. Jacky wondered just how they put back the big Lego. Would it be the same as the little ones he had?

Chapter 07

The moment Kirsten saw the crashed plane on the news, she made a direct line to the crash site. Despite Anna's warnings about going in pairs, Kirsten left the rest of her team working on their current case and drove down towards Dundee in an attempt to see if this incident was linked.

The evening was cool, and she drove through the dark while looking around in her rear-view mirror and side mirrors to see if she was tailed. However, Kirsten was determined not to be scared. Yes, there'd been an attack on her and on Craig, but she'd seen it coming and she needed to trust her instincts now as much as ever. Anna was going to work on that, work on who was coming after them. Kirsten's job was to deal with what was in front of them.

The crash site was evident and as Kirsten approached, the number of blue flashing lights were copious. She drove out to the line of the police, rolled down the window and showed her ID, which allowed her to get through into the inner cordon. From there, however, she had firemen blocking her path, advising that she needed to stay well clear. They pointed her over to an incident wagon that was parked at the side of a small forest road. The plane had come down within a wooded glen, making access to it difficult. According to the fireman she spoke to, the remnants of the plane had crashed and then slid down a verge, resting at the bottom, some sixty feet below from where the path was. Kirsten didn't need to get close to it, although she'd like to examine the site at some point. Instead, she made a beeline towards the incident van, knocked on the door, and found it being opened by a man in a suit.

'I'm Kirsten. I did phone ahead.'

'Ah, from the services,' said the man, and held the door open for her. 'The boss is still in the backroom just giving a briefing and asked that you wait here and hopefully, he'll be with you shortly.' Kirsten took a seat and waved her hand when the man offered her a coffee as she sat waiting. She watched numerous people file in and out of the room to her left, but then a familiar face stepped in from outside and planted herself on a seat beside Kirsten.

'Inspector Trawlish, I'm surprised you're here,' said Kirsten.

'Really? You don't think this could be linked? That's why you're here.'

'Well, if it's linked, why aren't you running it?' asked Kirsten.

'You've got a large crash site. You've got numerous services on board. The incident itself needs handling. I'm just looking for the connections. Inspector Woodrow will pass those to me when he's happy, but I take it that you're keen for that as well. We might as well go in together to speak to him.'

'He's in a briefing at the moment,' says Kirsten, 'but have you made any other headway?'

'None. Have you?'

'Not so far.'

'Well, I'd like to say I would trust you on that one, but with the way you guys work, who knows? Anyway, good to see you're all right.'

It took another five minutes before Inspector Woodrow was ready, and Kirsten and Inspector Trawlish were escorted into the room. It was the typical inside of an incident room, set out briefly with a bare table, a projection screen, numerous points for plugging in various devices. There was also a small desk at the side where Woodrow would set up his own laptop.

'Good to see you, Julia,' said the Inspector, shaking hands with Trawlish. 'And Kirsten—Stewart—isn't it? You were one of Macleod's, weren't you?'

Kirsten nodded. 'I left to join the darker side of what we do,' smiled Kirsten. 'I'm just wondering if we're all looking at the same case here.'

'Well, if you sit down, I'll tell you what I know.' The three sat down around the table and some coffee was brought through before Woodrow made sure the rest of the room was cleared as he spoke to the two women.

'From what we can gather, the aircraft was taken over. There was no distress call given about a hijack, but instead of following its flight plan, the aircraft began to descend. Numerous calls were made by air traffic to the aircraft, but none were responded to. They were in the process of scrambling fighter jets when the aircraft suddenly exploded, causing it to come down just outside where we are now. It hit the ground in a fireball. The main bulk of it, however, fell down a small ravine. It's a good thirty to fifty feet down there. We've got teams going down looking to extract who's down there, but as you can imagine, there was actually a fire to deal with in the first instance, so it's taken us a while.

'In terms of survivors,' said the man, 'we've no reports of any. We're getting the usual flood of phone calls saying that people saw the aircraft, but as far as we can gather, it just exploded. No one else has seen anything particularly untoward, or at least if they have, they haven't come to us with it. We're running a publicity campaign, trying to see if we can get more information, but as you understand, this thing takes time.'

'Have you been in touch with the operating company?' asked Kirsten.

'Queries have been made down south about that. It comes down from Biggin Hill where the company operates from. Like I said, our colleagues down south are picking up that angle.'

'Do you mind if I send someone down?' asked Kirsten.

Woodrow looked slightly offended. 'I'm sure the boys in London can do a good job,' he said.

'I'm sure they can,' said Kirsten, 'But we look for other things. If this was a hijack, we'll have to ask the question why? Secondly, what's the point of blowing up a plane if nobody gets off? Is it a simple act of terrorism or is there something else at play?'

'You mean what Julia's involved in?' asked Woodrow.

'Well, it's been a number of hours now,' said Inspector Trawlish, 'And so far, nobody's come forward. You still tracking down the company.'

'Yes,' said Woodrow, 'gone home, left the office.'

'But this will be all over the news,' said Trawlish. 'Why haven't they come forward? Why aren't they saying to us, 'That's our plane?''

'Like I say, the guys in London are tracing this now,' said Woodrow.

'Inspector Trawlish is right, though' said Kirsten. 'They should be coming forward screaming at us, 'That's our plane.

55

What happened?' but they're not. I don't understand that. Are we aware of any bodies on board?'

'From what we can see so far, there's two pilots in the cockpit. We haven't been able to get into the rest of it yet. One of the emergency doors has been taken off. It's not lying around close, but until we get down there properly and get into it, I can't say there's anyone inside.'

'What would the crew complement likely have been?' asked Trawlish.

'Who knows? You've probably got a capacity of taking up to ten. You're going to have a hostess or two in the back. Like I say, the London guys are picking all of that information up, but it should be coming this way very quickly.'

Kirsten thanked Woodrow for his information, and then suggested that Trawlish accompany her when they take a look at the crash site. The tall detective agreed and together, the two women walked as close as they could, stepping their way through the wood but noting the large expanse of trees that had been taken out by the crashed aircraft.

'You think this is tied in, don't you?' said Trawlish.

'Very much so. There are no other threats out about anyone looking to take over planes, but also, to take one over and blow it up is bizarre. There's been no feedback. No one's turned around and said, 'Look what we did.' Terrorist organisations are looking for publicity, looking to make a point, and if they're successful, they make that point by telling the news, the TV, the papers. They'll splash it everywhere, so why wouldn't you tell them?'

The two women walked along, the smell of fire in their nostrils and choking. By the time they made their way back to the incident van, there was a police constable waving at them.

'Inspector Trawlish, Inspector Woodrow would like you inside now. He has some information.'

'Good,' said Trawlish, undoing her coat and marching into the van. Kirsten followed, ignoring the constable's attempts to stop her.

'So, what have you got, Woodrow?' asked Trawlish, stepping inside.

'You're not going to believe this,' said Woodrow, 'Kirstie Macintyre was on that plane.'

'Kirstie Macintyre? Like- our Kirstie Macintyre, Scotland's finest, taking over the world down south, all over the TV and in the papers and in the press?'

'That one, exactly. I just took a call from the First Minister. She's found out about it as well. There's going to be a lot of press on this one.'

'I take it you haven't released it yet?'

'No, but it's going to come out. I've got a name, also, for the operating company. Mirage Aviation.'

'How many on board?' asked Kirsten.

'Five of them. The two pilots up the front, but there were also two flight attendants.'

'With the emergency door open, you think we would have found them. How far is your search around the area?'

'We've searched all around. We can't find anybody in a local area clear of the crash site itself. If anybody was thrown out, deftly opened the emergency hatch afterwards and stumbled out, they've not made it to anywhere. They'd also be looking to make contact, surely.'

'Not necessarily,' said Kirsten. 'It bugs me that that emergency door is open. The flight path, can you pull it up again?'

Inspector Woodrow turned round and started drawing on

a whiteboard, and Kirsten saw the descending profile of the plane at certain marks before the crash site.

'It was at a couple of thousand feet?'

'That's correct. Then after that, it drops out. We're not sure at what point the actual explosion took place, because that's the radar picture. We're not sure if they slipped out of radar cover or not. There was still a reasonable distance to run. Brief calculations would say that it probably exploded after that point where we lost contact.'

'It's up at forty-odd thousand feet and then all of a sudden, it comes down. It's coming down. How does it know it's not going to hit anything?'

'Highly unlikely,' said Inspector Woodrow, 'Up at that level, you're in the airways with planes coming back and forth from Scotland, but the time it starts coming down, there's not that much about. Sure, it's a calculated risk, but it was obvious to air traffic it still had its transponder on. They're going to turn things away, especially when they see that it's gone rogue.'

'And then it's down at the height where you can breathe okay, you could open the door without being too worried about it.'

'Are you thinking somebody jumped?' asked Trawlish.

Kirsten nodded. 'Exactly. Two attendants. If you're both from a terrorist faction, you could take over the aircraft. People who can get into the front cockpit, as I understand it,' said Kirsten, 'will be the crew.'

'They usually lock it during the flight, though don't they, until they land?'

'How well is that rule enforced on these types of flights, though? Is that more to do with commercial or does this classify as a commercial flight?'

'Kirstie Macintyre travels back and forward all the time. I

remember seeing a program on her,' said Trawlish. 'Basically, she lives down in London during the week, then she's back up here for the weekend. This is probably a routine thing. Are they going to be overly worried about locking anything?'

'If you'll excuse me,' said Woodrow, 'I need to organise telling her family what's going on, getting liaison organised, and keeping it quiet as well. No doubt, it'll get it to the press shortly, even if it doesn't come from us.'

'Of course,' said Kirsten, 'I'll give you some space, but I will be sending someone down to that company, Mirage Aviation. If I get anything, I'll speak to you.'

Trawlish followed Kirsten as she made her way back outside, and again took in the cloying breath of charred smoke, tree ash, and jet fuel.

'It's a bit crazy, isn't it?' said Trawlish. 'How many people do you know who could hijack a plane in that fashion, and get out? Who's doing this?'

'You'd have to be fairly professional to do that one. You don't just pitch up and go through it. If you're going to go in as the stewardesses or the stewards of the flight, how do you get in past security? How do you hold the details? I'm wondering if there's been extortion at the other end.'

'Really?' said Trawlish. 'You think it goes that deep?'

'Let me go on the phone. I've got a man who I know can find out.'

Kirsten made her way a short distance away from the incident room, finding a dark corner, before picking up her phone and calling Dom. She advised him of the incident and about Mirage Aviation, telling him and Carrie-Anne to get down to London as soon as possible. She gave them permission to go as deep as they wanted to find out what had happened, and advised that she wanted it done quickly.

When she put the phone down, she thought about Kirstie Macintyre, and she was absolutely prime for the case before her. They were talking about the execution of a celebrity. The things that Kirstie spoke about, they weren't really important, yet she had incredible focus, and for doing what? Did she really deserve to have all that attention, all that money lavished at her? Kirsten could see why some people would say no.

As she stood there with the floodlights behind her lighting up the crime sight, Kirsten saw many people walking back and forward. Most were dressed in police uniform, others were firefighters, and yet there were more from other services helping out as well. But it struck Kirsten, she was now standing here right in the open, on a dark night, and what's to stop anyone dressed as one of these workers coming up to her, somebody putting a bullet in her head. She needed to be smarter than this.

Kirsten made her way over to her car, stepped inside, and started the engine. For now, she was going to drive back up the road. They had a lead to chase. It would be up to Dom and Carrie-Anne in the morning to sort that out.

Chapter 08

The following morning, Dom picked up Carrie-Anne and they made their way to the airport, catching an early morning flight down to London. From there, they hired a car out to Biggin Hill, the origin of the destroyed flight, seeking out Mirage Aviation. The woman at the front desk pointed to a unit on the far side of the airfield saying to gain access from there, but the police were already there and speaking to the company.

On arrival at the police, Dom felt he was being fobbed off. A young constable was sent out to talk to them, advising that their detective inspector was currently speaking to the owner. Dom tried to push in, but the constable was insistent. Carrie-Anne put a hand on Dom's shoulder.

'Maybe we should try somebody else within the company. The managing director is going to be locking things down tight, desperate to keep away any issues that are going on. Let's see if the secretary's available.'

Dom asked the constable if they could go inside and speak to the other staff and he said it was okay, as long as he accompanied them. The pair made their way through to an office where staff were sitting around, almost in shock.

'Which one of you here makes up the duty rosters and the flights?'

'That would be me,' said a woman.

'Good,' said Dom. 'We need to speak to you.' He led the woman over to the far corner. Carrie-Anne smiled at her, trying to relax her, but she could see the woman's hands were shaking.

'What's your name, love?' asked Carrie-Anne.

'Anita. I'm not that long in here, have only been working three months. This is terrible. She was one of the big customers, Kirstie Macintyre.'

'It doesn't mean she's dead yet,' said Dom. 'Until we know for sure, let's try and keep an open mind. Now, can you tell me which staff were actually on that day? Not the two pilots, we know about them, but the flight attendants, who were they?'

'Well, that's the thing, our regulars, they weren't available, so we got some agency staff. It was hard at such short notice because it was literally an hour before they wanted to take off and I had to use it, an agency I had only just heard about.'

'In what way?' asked Carrie-Anne.

'Well, they'd come around touting, looking for business, said they're just starting up. The way things have been there's agency staff hiring out there, but obviously, you need to have all the paperwork signed off and these guys just seemed to fall into my lap.'

Dom looked over at Carrie-Anne. 'And the agency you got these people from?' asked Dom.

'Edie's Flight Crew. They've got an address on the other side of Biggin Hill. It's a small office actually, just up above the self-shops. They didn't have class and I hadn't used them before, but we were in dire need and they were the only ones who could get us someone quick. In fact, they came touting for business just after the others had phoned in sick.'

'Did they?' said Dom. 'That's interesting. Give us the address, it'd be much appreciated.' Dom watched Anita disappear, then grabbed a pen and paper and started writing down an address with a post code.

'When you said that they just kind of happened to be calling around, did you feel you had any choice but to go with them?'

'Well, no, because as we say, Kirstie Macintyre, she's like the big name. She's the one we have to be ready for. We moved heaven and earth, but the other flights seemed to be out of the way.'

'You had no spare planes?'

'No,' said Anita.

'Can you give me the other flight details?' asked Carrie-Anne. 'The other ones that were operating?'

As Anita disappeared, Dom looked at her with a questioning face.

'I just want to see if anybody bought up those flights, made sure.'

'It's a good idea,' said Dom. 'Somebody made sure that there were no planes available. They had to go with the current staff.' After a few minutes, Anita came back with the details and the pair decided they would leave, since the likelihood of getting to speak to the managing director seemed minimal.

They took the hire car to the other side of Biggin Hill, and identified from the shop fronts that were in front of the correct office building. As they got close, Dom looked up at the window above and saw a woman racing around her office. Carrie-Anne and Dom climbed the stairs, which were wooden, so it was hard to disguise their arrival. As they reached the top, a door opened, and a woman raced out.

'Can I just stop you a moment?' said Carrie-Anne, putting her arm across and making sure that the woman was indeed stopped. 'We're looking for someone from Edie's Flight Crew. I noticed you'd just come out of that door. Would you be the owner?'

'Why? Who wants to know?'

'We're with the special side of the police,' said Carrie-Anne. 'We're trying to make inquiries discreetly. Please, just turn around and go back in for us.'

Carrie-Anne turned the woman back around and almost manhandled her back into the office where Dom closed the door behind them. The woman was of medium build and height with nothing particularly distinctive about her. Her auburn hair was done up in a bun at the back and she wore a plain smart suit, but her face had a guilty look about it.

'We just want to ask about the crew you lent out to Mirage Aviation yesterday. We'd like some details on who they were.'

The woman looked across at her desk and Dom clocked that she was looking at a picture of some kids. She answered back, 'I'm not too sure I can give out details of that sort.'

'We're the sort of people you have to give that detail to; otherwise, we talk to you at a station about it,' said Carrie-Anne.

'I can't. There were a couple jobs in. We got them sorted, I think it's just—'

The woman seemed to be jabbering here, there, and everywhere saying several different names. Then she started to get defensive. 'Look, if you need to get the names, then I need a warrant. I need you to come back and tell me. Otherwise, you're just going to have to arrest me now and take me in.'

'Arrest you?' queried Carrie-Anne. 'Nobody said arrest.'

'But we can take you in,' said Dom. 'In fact, I think we should do that right now.'

Carrie-Anne stepped across Dom, turned and looked at him, but in a weird voice said, 'Better make sure of the paperwork on this one; we don't want to get caught out.' Dom looked at Carrie-Anne's face, questioning, but Carrie-Anne gave him a wink with one eye.

'You're right. We'll be back shortly with our warrant. Don't go anywhere, Miss.'

'Warner. In fact, it's Mrs.'

'Well, Mrs Warner, don't leave the country. Don't leave town, we'll be back shortly. We expect to see you in this office this afternoon.'

Carrie-Anne and Dom left the building by the stairs and sat in their car across the street. It took five minutes before the woman exited the building, made her way to a small Mini, and began to drive along the main village street. Dom casually followed her in the hire car.

Mrs Warner drove out of the village further into the countryside where Dom saw her turn into a forest car park. The day was becoming overcast with a light drizzle, but he watched as she parked up, before taking his own car to the far side of the car park. From there in the rear-view mirror, he watched her sitting anxiously, looking around the car park.

After ten minutes, a van drove in, grey in colour, and pulled up alongside Mrs Warner's Mini. The door was slid back and Mrs Warner stepped out of her vehicle and was quickly bundled into the van. The sliding door was shut.

Dom and Carrie-Anne sat and watched the van pull out of the car park and disappear off down the road before they followed quickly behind. This time, Don kept at a good distance, worried that those in the van might be more adept at seeing if people were following them than Mrs Warner had been. The van looked slightly beat up, but the sound of the engine was true.

Don watched as it turned into an industrial state before driving past a large, fenced building, where the gate was quickly opened, and the van pulled inside. Dom cut off the road before he reached the building, stopping out of sight behind another factory. Quickly, the pair got out of the car and made their way around the back of that factory to look at the gate from a different angle.

They could see someone on watch, but behind them, the grey van had its side door open. Mrs Warner was taken out with a black hood over her head. She was quickly taken inside the factory and Dom and Carrie-Anne watched for a moment, until the man on the gate disappeared inside the building as well.

'If we come in from the far side,' said Carrie-Anne. 'We might get a look in. Do you want to go or shall I?'

'We go together. Kirsten's orders. Whoever goes in the room would be out of sight from the other. With the other things that are going on, best we stay in pairs.' Carrie-Anne nodded and the pair made their way around the far side of the factory building, where they'd seen Mrs Warner go. There, with a high gate in front of them, Dom gave Carrie-Anne a foot up and she was able to grab the top and throw herself over. Dom then climbed to get himself up before he dropped down on the other side.

The pair ran across an empty car park to the building. Once they got close, they were able to look inside a window and see a large expanse inside. In the middle of that expanse were a few children sitting in a circle with Mrs Warner beside them. A number of men with guns stayed around the outside of the circle, mainly looking out, rather than in. Dom tried to keep low beside the window.

'Do we make a move here?' asked Carrie-Anne.

Dom looked around him, 'No,' he said. 'This is too great a risk. They've got everyone around the kids at the moment. We move in, they can just turn around and kill them, Mrs Warner too. We know where these guys are. The best thing to do is to keep a watching brief, maybe even get some company to go in.'

'Given the people that have been watching us and tried to take a pot shot before, if they are anything to do with these people, I'd say we'd be better going in alone later,' said Carrie-Anne. 'You can see why the woman's scared, though. It's no wonder the police force hasn't traced her yet.'

'I doubt our kidnappers are talking to the managing director, not involved up to the top. Maybe Kirstie Macintyre isn't such a big deal here,' whispered Dom.

Together they edged around the building, made their way inside and slowly climbed up some steps, which took them to a higher floor. However, the interior of the building was hollow and from high up, they were able to look down at the circle of children and the nervous mother with them. Mrs Warner stayed with them for about an hour before she made her way back to the car.

'Do we follow?' asked Carrie-Anne.

'No,' said Dom. 'Let's see what these guys do.'

From their high-up position, they were able to see the men start to take shifts. There was a separate room off to one side that the men seemed to go into, leaving only one person in charge of the children. In truth, the children didn't look like they were going to do anything, scared witless, and with a man with a gun in front of them.

'You could rush in,' whispered Carrie-Anne.

'No,' said Dom. 'When we do it, we need to go in and take out that other room first. Someone up here, take out the man that's watching the kids. We have to be clean and quick. I think it's best being left to nightfall.'

As they made their way back down the steps and then to the rear of the building, they once again jumped the gate before walking slowly around the rear side of the factory. The car was parked on the other side. As they came close to the car, Carrie-Anne held back. Someone was up close to it, and they waited, watching until a car pulled up and the person disappeared in it.

'That's a bit strange,' said Carrie-Anne.

'Indeed, it is,' said Dom. 'You don't go near a car for ten minutes. Let's sweep out wide, make sure nobody's watching it.'

Together, the pair ran off into other factories that were linked to the one the car was parked beside. They sought to see if anyone was about, but the area was abandoned, and all industrial buildings seemed to no longer be in use. Once they were sure that there was no one else near their car, they made their way back to it. Carrie-Anne went to open the door.

'No,' said Dom. 'Wait!' He got down onto his back on the road and shuffled slowly underneath the vehicle.

'It's crude, it's basic, easy to disable, but if we'd driven off, that car would've got launched into the air. There's a small tilt on this.'

'What do you mean, a small tilt?' asked Carrie-Anne.

Dom shuffled out from under the car, holding in his hand a small bomb.

'Is that what I think it is?' asked Carrie-Anne.

'Indeed, it is,' said Dom. 'I'm phoning this one in. It's okay, I've made it safe. Like I say, it was very quickly rigged up. They obviously didn't spend a lot of time on the car, and they didn't want to watch it either.'

'I didn't see us being tailed today. Did you?'

'No,' said Dom. 'And yet here we are. I just wonder if they were involved in this kidnap or is it somebody else.'

Dom took a further look around the car, opening up the bonnet, checking out the engine and once he was happy it was clear, they quickly drove off deciding not to return to Edie's Flight Crew that afternoon. Now they knew who their target was, they would wait at a distance before coming back that evening.

Chapter 09

Carrie-Anne sat in her black clothing with a black balaclava pulled over her face and her hair tied up in a knot behind her head. She pulled her gloves over her bare hands, then checked her weapon, attaching the silencer. She looked across at Dom who was doing the same before they stepped out of the car which was parked behind a factory in full view of the area they were going to. They had completed their return back to where they saw the children being held hostage and were ready to make their attack to free Mrs Warner's kids. However, as they left their digs, Dom thought they were being followed, but despite weaving in and out of traffic, he couldn't locate what was bothering him. After a short consultation, they decided they were going to continue with the plan. Carrie-Anne knew the pressure she was now going to be under.

'Are you sure about this, Dom? We could call for more backup.'

'They'd get seen and scare these people off. If we arrive in a large group, it's always the same. No, the two of us together, nice and easy, kids in the car, and get out of here. Get everyone down to the police station afterwards. The inspector down here will give us a warm thank you, anyway.'

'They'll be on to Mrs Warner by now, won't they?' asked Carrie-Anne.

'Undoubtedly,' said Dom, 'if they start charging around, who knows what's going to happen? No, we need to go in and get these kids. Once we do that, we can disappear back up north.'

Quietly, they left their car, and walked outside of the streetlight around to the factory they were aiming to infiltrate. The gate where Mrs Warner entered earlier in the day had a light above it, but the other gate they'd climbed over previously that evening was in the dark on the far side of the factory.

Once again, Dom gave Carrie-Anne a lift up and she flung herself over the top. She covered the ground around her while Dom climbed the fence. Quickly, they ran around the perimeter before entering the building. Once inside, Dom stopped, looking out behind him while Carrie-Anne made sure the way ahead was clear, but there was no one following them, nor looking out.

'Let's get up the stairs,' said Dom. Slowly they crept back up to the position they'd occupied earlier on that day. From the high vantage point, they were able to look down and see three kids asleep on the floor, one man standing over them, idly puffing on a cigarette. There was a light hanging over the kids but otherwise, the interior of the factory was unlit except for a beam coming out from the side office where most of the men had been stationed earlier that day.

'Good to go,' said Carrie-Anne.

Dom nodded. 'Just keep him covered. First sign of trouble, take him out.'

Carrie-Anne looked down at the man standing by the kids and aimed right at the man's head.

Dom took the stairs back down before slowly moving along the outside of the building until he got level with where the office would be. The light was on, and he could see it shining out into the car park, but he stayed close by the windows, listening. He wasn't sure, but he thought he could hear a football match on. Maybe they had a recording because there wouldn't be anything live in England at this time of night. After all, it was one in the morning. Maybe it was some foreign league. *All the better though*, thought Dom as he turned back until he found the door into the building.

He opened it slowly, stepped inside, and saw a corridor in front of him. Quietly, he walked the length of the corridor before finding another door. There was a small window in it. He peeped through to see a figure in the hallway beyond. A little further on, he saw lights. Dom reckoned he must be close now to the office where the men were resting. He'd have to be quick with this guy, take him out, remove him or else go straight on into the office. What he didn't like about that was he could be going into the office blind. Dom decided instead he would take the man out, hide him, and then creep up on the office.

Slowly, he turned the handle of the door while peeping up into the window and ascertaining where the man was. The man looked towards the window and Dom leaned back. When he glanced through again, the man had his back to the door. Opening it quickly and keeping one foot on the door to keep it ajar, Dom reached up, grabbed the man's head and neck, and snapped it. He pulled the man back through the doorway, allowing the door to close gently without making a sound.

Once he checked that he had fully incapacitated the guard, Dom made his way back through the door, creeping up along the wall before looking inside the window. There were six men in there. Dom realised he wouldn't be able to get inside and shoot them all before they reacted. He thought about what he should do instead.

Reaching inside his jacket, he pulled out two flashbangs, devices that when he threw them into the room, would give off a blinding light and a deafening sound, hopefully freezing the men from reacting for several seconds. He'd have to be turned away while they went off and then he'd need to enter quickly, take out all six men before making his way out to grab the children and run. This would take time, but Dom thought it might be the only way to incapacitate all the men at once.

He looked in through the window again. They were all sitting with beer, watching a movie. Dom finally recognised it as *The Great Escape*. That's where the football noises were coming from. A sudden thought ran through his head. *What would be the film that he would like to watch if he was getting taken out? What would be the last film to flash before his eyes?* He didn't know; in truth, he didn't watch many and hadn't been to the cinema in a long time.

He should do that, he thought. He should ask Carrie-Anne to the cinema because if he did and things weren't great between them or things didn't go in any way he wished, it could always just be two colleagues on a night out, call it a *works do*.

Dom looked inside again and decided the best way to set his flashbangs off was to open the door and slide the first one in, before throwing another one in through one of the glass windows further up the corridor. From there, it would land in front of the TV while the other one would be landing behind them, so whatever way they were facing, they would get hit with the blinding light and the loud bang.

Dom glided up to the window he would have to break, took a quick look to check its integrity and decided that the butt of his gun would break it reasonably easily. With that in mind, he turned, made his way back to the door of the small office and opened it. One flashbang was in his hand and he tossed it into the office before turning on his heel and running back down the corridor. His gun, in the other hand, then connected with the window. There was the sound of breaking glass. He launched a second flashbang through, covering his ears and making his way back down to the doorway.

There was a loud explosion. Dom could see the light flashing out through the windows. The second explosion came a moment later and Dom entered the room and saw the men throwing their hands up towards their ears. He fired twice, then again, then a third time, then a fourth and a fifth. He heard gunfire from outside, a single shot. Then he fired another one as he saw someone try to reach for his gun.

Dom looked at all of the men in front of him, now lying on the ground, and quickly ran around each of them checking that they wouldn't be getting back up again. The sound of a goal being scored in the TV now seemed deafening. As he exited the door into the large warehouse, he saw a body lying there and children now woken up and screaming. Dom looked left and right then ran over.

'It's okay. It's okay. I'm here to get you. Mum sent me. Mum sent me; I'm here to take you away. Give me your hand.' said Dom. He grabbed what looked like the oldest child's hand. The child couldn't have been more than about eight. He told the younger ones to grab hold hands. When the kids saw his gun, however, they started backing away from him.

'It's okay,' said Dom, putting his hands to the air. 'I'm here to help you. This isn't for you. This is for anyone that gets in our way. I'm here to help you. Please be calm. Be calm.' Dom saw the youngest child scream at him, and he put his hands up saying, 'No, no, it's okay.' Then he saw a finger being pointed. He spun and saw behind him two figures, one raising a gun.

There came two quick shots from high above. Each of the figures fell to the ground and Dom pulled out his gun, sending a second bullet into each. Behind him, the kids screamed. He picked up the smallest one and then yelled at the eldest to grab the other one and told them to start running.

They were afraid, panicked, but someone had issued down an instruction, and he heard them following him. He made his way back through the office, telling the kids not to look back along the corridor as they passed yet another body. Then he was met by Carrie-Anne at the foot of the steps. She picked up the second youngest, urging the eldest to run with them and together, they made their way out towards the gate at the back. This time, Dom shot the lock off, kicked the gate open and continued to run.

As they got round to the rear of the factory, Dom put his child down, telling Carrie-Anne to look after him. He ran up to the car, rolling himself onto the ground to look underneath. He then raced round to the front, pulled open the driver's door, and sprung the bonnet, before looking in at the engine.

'Get them in,' he said. 'Carrie-Anne, get them in.' Quickly, she opened the rear door and started ushering the children inside. Dom jumped into the driver's seat and Carrie-Anne got into the rear with the children. As Dom pulled away in the car, he heard a screeching of tyres.

'Behind us,' he said, 'Carrie-Anne, there's people behind us.'

She grabbed the children, pushing them, driving their heads

down. Dom could hear gunfire from the other car, but he was quick onto the accelerator. He pulled away, driving at pace around corners. None of the children had seat belts on, but with Carrie-Anne lying over them, Dom drove as quick as he could.

Meanwhile, Carrie-Anne was on the phone calling Justin Chivers.

'Justin, extraction. Need safe house location near Beacon Hill. One with a welcome party, somewhere I can go to. We're being pursued. Have children on board.'

'Just a moment,' said Justin, his voice as calm as anything. Carrie-Anne looked across at Dom at the wheel, but the man was focused intently, driving out now into traffic. The vehicle behind them was following, but no longer was there gunfire. Dom ran a red light, causing the car coming from his right to swerve, spin, and crash into a lamppost, but the pursuing car continued. Carrie-Anne sat with her hands over the children's heads and started muttering to herself, *Come on, Justin, come on. Where? Where?*

She heard a beep on her phone; with another couple of presses, a route was coming up on her map's function, giving her a way to safety. She called out from the back of the car, 'Next left.'

Dom saw a set of red lights ahead, but he ignored them, spinning around into the traffic that was already crossing, sending several people diving out of the way. The car behind was hot on his heels and he watched it in his rear mirror, cursing it. He could see a flash of lights as well starting up behind him.

'Blues, there's police.'

'Justin, we have police in pursuit, tell them to back off, get them off. Right, Dom, right,' shouted Carrie-Anne.

It was an L-shaped right-hand bend that Dom had to take, but he lifted the handbrake and the car slid round and then roared on, the poor hire car having never taken this sort of punishment in its life. It was being driven flat out for all it was worth.

The roads started to lead out into the country and after another five minutes of pursuit, Dom could see that there were no blue lights following them. However, the other car was still there.

'Next one on the right. Look for the large farm building,' shouted Carrie-Anne.

Dom careered over a corner, his wing mirror clipping a tree on the side and disappearing. The car bounced down a rugged track, but he saw the building up ahead, the large barn doors of which were being opened. He drove inside and then out through some doors at the rear. Behind him, the pursuing car drove through the double doors, suddenly found its tyres being shredded and the doors ahead of it being shut quickly. It crashed and was descended upon by a number of figures, all with guns.

Dom brought his own car to a halt. Carrie-Anne could hear the sobbing of kids underneath her grip, and she slowly got upright, before lifting the kids up and then holding them tight.

'You okay?' asked Dom.

'Good driving,' she said. 'Thank God, Dom—good driving.'

Chapter 10

Anna Hunt stepped out of the office of the Chief Constable and made her way out of the building into a waiting car. She nodded at the driver, and he took off through the streets of London heading for a remote location known only to a few people. As she watched the famous landmarks go past, Anna caught a glimpse of the London Eye and saw it slowly rotating on and on. That's what was happening, wasn't it? A knock-on effect from the other, no way to stop it, everything continuing to spin, continuing to come around again.

As she looked down at the files sitting beside her in the car, she focused on the woman in the photograph on the front page. In the picture, she had long, brunette hair. That's not the way Anna remembered her. She had seen the body brought back from Scotland and autopsied in the London headquarters of her service. They wanted to confirm who it was, wanted to confirm that she was definitely dead, and this was not some imposter.

After some digging, the DNA from that body was found to be matched to a rare piece of DNA picked up by a field agent out in Russia. At the time, it had seemed an innocuous grab. A woman invited back to a man's apartment, a few drinks, and some skin samples picked up in the middle of the night as she lay sleeping in the man's bed. Those samples taken from so long ago were now holding a key to a bigger mystery: Why were Anna's agents being targeted.

As they drove through the countryside, Anna sat back in her seat and looked out at the blue sky, misleadingly giving the impression it was warm outside. However, the temperatures were still cool. The heating in the car was on, and Anna took her jacket off, relishing the warmth.

The car took a turn through a small village, then drove to a farm, parking up inside a shed beside a farmhouse. Once there, Anna stepped out of her car with her belongings. Calmly, she made her way over to a small corner of the shed where a lift descended into the ground. She descended three or four levels before the lift stopped. Then she stepped out putting her hand up to a reader which confirmed her fingerprints. Her eye was then scanned before the door opened and she stepped into a busy office.

The centre of the room was filled with many desks and people talking on phones, looking at screens filled with images and data, coordinators looking at various operations within the country. This was where her agency operated from and she could see at the far end, the dominant office where Godfrey was standing up inside, looking across the room at her.

She gave a brief nod and made for a smaller office on the edge of the room, stepping across the immaculate white floor. Her own office was not so bright, with dark, brown colours and a carpet that allowed her to take her shoes off and place her feet into the plushness of it.

Sitting down, she placed a video link call to Inverness and

to the desk of Kirsten Stewart. Anna hung her jacket up and sat down awaiting the answer on her laptop. It was a few moments—background systems were running and making sure that secure lines were set up—before the screen appeared.

Kirsten was sitting before Anna with a sweatshirt on and her hair splayed out behind her. Anna had always thought that Kirsten was small but perfectly formed. Fit as a fiddle, but also had a look about her that Kirsten could never see. Carrie-Anne, in her office, was tall, elegant, with a lot of style of about her. Kirsten had that homely look, the one that Anna fought hard to compliment. In some ways, she wasn't like an agent. If Anna hadn't been looking through the police files for recruits, she probably wouldn't have come across her. But Macleod had known and Anna Hunt was darn glad that he had.

'Have you heard from Dom and Carrie-Anne?' asked Kirsten.

'We've been helping the police tidy up. We've put a lockdown over the whole incident, but the good news is that they're both well. They also managed to escape with three children who were being held and we're beginning to see what happened with the flight.'

Kirsten nodded, lifted her coffee cup to her mouth, swilling it round her mouth before putting it down, but with eyes focused on Anna. It seemed she was ready. Anna Hunt continued her story.

'Kirstie Mackenzie boarded the flight, but the normal flight attendants were not available. Someone had got to them and made them ill, but they had phoned in nearly an hour before the flight was due to take off. Around the same time, a new agency was phoning Mirage Aviation telling them they had people available on short notice. It seemed too good to be true and two attendants were placed onto the flight. However, the agency in question, Edie's Flight Crew, had been intimidated. The lady who organised the flight rotas had her children kidnapped and held hostage while she then proffered the new attendants onto that flight.'

'So, we don't think that the attendants were on it when it went down. We think they planted the bomb?'

'Exactly,' said Anna, 'but more than that, we think they took Kirstie Macintyre.'

'That's not easy to do, is it?' said Kirsten. 'They're going to have to know how to operate an aircraft, set the autopilot, decide when to jump out, check their navigation. They have to be able to parachute, they have to be able to take Kirstie hostage with them and jump with her, know when to open the emergency door.'

'Exactly, but I'm thinking they're mercenaries.'

'What about those who were holding the kids hostage?' asked Kirsten.

'That was the thing; Dom and Carrie-Anne dispatched them all. When we got them back, they were mercenaries, but not of the same calibre. These were pretty low-level guys from our own country. Not people I'd be hiring for a particularly big job. Also, they seem to be disposable.'

'I was getting worried that there was somebody else.'

'Dom was being watched as he reported to you. They followed protocol and kept Dom active on the ground with Carrie-Anne observing from high up. She took down two people who arrived late to the party. We checked out who they were and both of them have links to a woman known only as The Huntress. She operates out of Russia. We've got no pictures of her; she's just a name, almost a legend. What we know is from DNA searches that we've done before, and her DNA seems to be linked to Control. We don't believe it's the same woman, obviously, because Control was dead, but there's a definite connection, possibly family.

'I think this is a revenge attack. Someone's coming for you and the team. Craig, possibly me as well. They certainly went after you both. I think it's sensible you keep up the pairs, don't let anybody out on their own, and don't go out in the open unless necessary.'

'Why don't we switch the team? Why don't you get one of the other teams to cover this job off? We can go dark until we can find this Huntress and finish her off.'

'I haven't got anybody available,' said Anna. 'Besides you won't find her, she'll find you. That's the way this plays out.'

'So, my people have to operate with a target on their backs at the same time as being out, trying to prevent whatever this group is, that seem to want to kill off celebrities.'

'That's the long and the short of it,' said Anna. 'The problem I'm having is how are they able to find you so easily? How are they tailing you? What's going on? There may be a leak from inside, not necessarily from headquarters, but from someone, someone attached to our service or elsewhere.'

'I'm going to be speaking to the inspector running the operation around the aircraft crash. Trawlish will be there as well; maybe I'll be able to get more information about how it was done, maybe get better links into this group. You don't think they're tied, do you? Those coming after us and this group?'

'I doubt it,' said Anna. 'I really doubt it. The agenda seems so very different, but I do think someone knows what you're doing. That's how they're getting a tail on you. I'm going to speak to Godfrey. We don't like it when we've got rogue people within our organisation, however loosely attached they are. I'll get onto that, and you keep going, find whoever's taking these celebrities. There'll be a clock on it, remember. At some point, it'll be their execution day; the brochure says that much.'

'Are there any extra precautions you can give us?' asked Kirsten. 'Any extra bodies you can send to us, maybe a few guards on the street below?'

'No,' said Anna. 'Keep it quiet, keep it internal, and don't let them see you rattled. You've got to be careful until we see how much they actually know. Leave the purging of this to me and Godfrey; we know what to do. After the last time when he brought you in to the inner circle meeting, I can see why you're a target. Ultimately, the Huntress would want to destabilise us as an organisation, take out Godfrey, but he's hard to get to. At the moment, it looks like you're top dog, ready for picking.'

'Well, I look forward to that,' said Kirsten. 'I need to go and meet with these inspectors.'

'Okay,' said Anna. 'Kirsten, stay safe, stay aware, and don't be afraid to shoot first.'

The video call closed, and Anna knew that Kirsten wouldn't feel good about the last comment. Kirsten never shot first. She always made sure she was doing the right thing, the one flaw in her, as Anna saw it.

Anna stood up and made her way out of her office, and over towards Godfrey's. She stood outside the glass panelling, as she could see he had somebody in with him. The glass was soundproof, for nobody got to hear what was going on inside Godfrey's office. Anna waited for two minutes before she saw a wave, inviting her in. A dark-haired man left at the same time but held the door open for Anna. She had never seen him before, but that wasn't unusual with visitors to Godfrey's office.

'Miss Hunt, always good to see you.' Anna noticed that the door hadn't closed behind her yet, and she turned to see the man standing and looking at Godfrey. Godfrey gave a little nod and the man stood outside his office.

'Who's that?'

'Apologies, Anna, I kept it formal. He's my bodyguard at the moment. I just thought I'd take an extra precaution.'

'I don't recognise him.'

'Good,' said Godfrey, 'because your memory's good and you'd recognise anybody I've been with. Nobody in here knows him. He doesn't know anybody in here; he'll treat everyone as if they are a threat, even you, Anna.'

'As it should be. I take it you've seen the message?'

'The Huntress. I used to think she was a legend, but not anymore. Are you sure it's wise to keep your team operating?'

'Well, we do have a slight situation on our hands up in Scotland; besides, if we put another team on it, they'll find out they're from us. I think she'll just dispatch them. Kirsten and her group can handle this; she's good, wise, clever for her age. We need to call her out, get the Huntress out in front of us. We need to put an end to her once and for all. She's been moving things in the background on the Russian front for a long time. Suddenly, she's made it personal; suddenly, she's coming out. We need to go for her.'

'You definitely think the link to what you're doing and why she's able to follow your people is because of someone inside the organisation? Do you have any evidence of that?' asked Godfrey.

'You know if I had, I would've put it in my report.'

'Well, I was thinking in case it was something too close, too personal, something that you wouldn't want to go down on a note.'

'It's just a hunch,' said Anna. 'I mean, they could do it from observation, but they surprised Dom and Carrie-Anne. These people are good, really good. The operations they're involved in aren't seen by that many people. It shouldn't be that difficult to weed someone out if someone is passing on information, and it'll be from this room; you know that, don't you, Godfrey? We're clean up north, very clean.'

'Oh, I have no doubt of that, but always keep an open mind, Anna. I shall make the enquiries, but when I find out who it is, I will let you have a word. I want you to then follow the trail. I have bigger things to handle, I can't be side-tracked.'

'Of course,' said Anna. 'Besides, it should be me. It's my team they're coming after. Do you want her?'

'Only if you can capture her safely. If you can't, you are free to use whatever measures that are necessary. But be warned, if she is linked to Control, she won't be easy to get. Control, last time, got close to me. So close and nobody saw it.'

'Except Kirsten,' said Anna. 'That's why you brought her in. That's why you need her to do this.'

Godfrey nodded. 'That's why I don't like this risk; it feels like we're dangling her as bait, her and her team. Meanwhile, they've got these celebrities to deal with. This could go messy, very messy.'

'It always could be messy. The train station in London, we were two metres from messy. It's what Kirsten does well; she's not a refined spy, but she's dogged. Find me the leak, please, Godfrey. I'll be there once you know who it is.'

Anna gave a nod and made her way to the door where the dark-haired man opened it for her. She could feel his eyes staring at her, as she made her way back to her office. This was the hard bit. She had played her pieces, Kirsten was off chasing the celebrities, Godfrey was now chasing the leak. Anna would have to be patient, but when it came, when her time arrived, she would be deadly.

Chapter 11

Kirsten left the office and walked down to her car, glancing across the street at all times. She still remembered the car charging down the street, taking a shot at Craig, and lying there behind the car with him while shots rained above them. This time, there was no such drama and she stepped into her vehicle. She happily turned on the engine and drove off uptown to the police station across from the hospital.

Parking the car at the rear, Kirsten took the staff entrance, choosing not to come in through the front and give someone a bird's eye view of what she was doing. Instead, once inside, she made her way up three floors, turned a corner to the office of Inspector Trawlish who was sitting behind her desk with a wry smile on her face. 'You could have tuned in through your laptop. You didn't have to come in and sit with me personally.'

'No, but this way, it's all done on your communications. It's not seen as being sent out to ourselves. Secondly, I prefer to operate within the room. It's easier talking face to face, especially when it's so easy to tread on each other's toes.'

'Well, you'll need to tread away because quite frankly, up at my end, we've got nothing. I haven't been able to trace anyone involved with Mr Argyle's kidnap, and now, this one has occurred as well. It feels like we're aiming at ghosts in the mist—nothing's come up at all. Except I know Inspector Woodrow has got something for me. He wouldn't tell, but there was an excitement in his voice when he rang.'

'That's all well and good,' said Kirsten, 'as long as it gets us near.'

'By the way, are you all right?' asked Trawlish.

'I'm fine, why?'

'Little shooting incident the other day.'

'Thank you. Nice of you to ask, but I'm fine.'

It did feel like she was asking out of concern, thought Kirsten. *Wasn't one of those fishing questions, trying to find out more.* When Kirsten closed the conversation, Trawlish didn't try and reopen it and take her down a path she didn't want to go.

'Well, it's almost time. Let's put the call through,' said Trawlish. Thirty seconds later, the face of Inspector Woodrow dominated the screen across the room.

'Julia, it's good to see you.'

'Just to let you know, Inspector Woodrow, I've got Kirsten from the other services here.'

'All right, I didn't realise that, Inspector Trawlish; we'll get to it then.'

Kirsten could see that the two knew each other well, although she couldn't judge if it was more than just simple professional courtesy that they dropped the first names as soon as Woodrow knew that Kirsten was in the room.

'The good news is that we haven't been able to find any more bodies. We've hunted all over the crash site and beyond, but there are none.'

'Could they have gone up in the explosion though?' asked

Kirsten.

'Well, of course, they could. Always an option, although the type of explosion it was, forensics say, we'd expect at least to find some body parts, but we found none. Only the two bodies of the pilots. The other information that's come to light though, is that parachutes were seen from a distance.'

'How many?' asked Kirsten.

'That's the thing,' said Woodrow. 'Only the two, we've got three potential people in there, but only two parachutes.'

'Unless this is a kidnap,' said Kirsten. 'You only need the two, tie the victim to one of them, jump out of the plane, land somewhere, get picked up on the move before anybody's reacted. Everybody else is racing towards the large explosion and the crash site. Why did it take so long for the parachute information to come through?' asked Kirsten.

'Presumably because we were canvassing the wrong area. The report about it came through second-hand as well because it was over water or presumed to be over water by the person watching. They called the Coastguard. The Coastguard called it in, of course, but we were in the middle of dealing with a crashed aircraft. It didn't get too far up the chain until someone, when reviewing it, realised it was very important information—fed it through.'

'You have a location for where these parachutes were?'

'It was very loose,' said Woodrow. 'The trouble was that the original sighting that said there were parachutes came from far away. They didn't see them at a great height. We then put out a request for other sightings in an expanding area, and a father came back saying his kid had seen them up in the air with a big plane. He said, 'When the kid pointed it wasn't low, it was high,' so they must have been near enough over the top if they worked out from there.'

'Do you have a grid reference for those sightings?' asked Kirsten. Woodrow passed the information, and she made a note ready to send it to Justin Chivers.

'What's your move from here?' asked Trawlish.

'Well, we're doing a bit more canvasing, see if anybody has seen anything. Obviously, if this was a kidnap, and I have a very open mind on that, you would have to take away the victim as well as wrap up those parachutes.'

'You'd also have to land your parachute somewhere sensible,' said Kirsten, 'near a road to enable a quick getaway. No point landing in a large field where there's are no roads, and then have to carry your victim with you. You want to be landing, picking her up, and dumping her in the back of a van.'

'You sound like you've done this before,' said Woodrow. 'Do you ever employ this tactic?'

'No,' said Kirsten. 'What I do know, if London's moving a bit slow for you, is that the two flight attendants on that flight were not who they're meant to be. The normal ones were poisoned or made ill in some way. An employee of an agency, who specialised in delivering flight crew on a quick notice, had children being held, and then had to put forward two other flight attendants. I believe they were actually mercenaries, and we are working to try and trace that through. I told you this earlier, but two of my team had to go and rescue those children. They've got them out alive, thankfully, but we've got a lot of dead bodies and we're sifting through who's who. Those that were left behind were certainly mercenaries. However, we do have these two other flight attendants that are unaccounted for.'

'What's your thoughts?' asked Trawlish to Kirsten.

'Well, have you got a map?'

Trawlish nodded and produced a map on the table in front of Kirsten. She ran her finger along the grid references, pinpointing where the sighting had been. From there, she started looking around for available touchdown sites for the parachutes.

'You're going to want to jump out and get to ground quick. Obviously, you've got to break the fall to some degree, or you smash your legs, but outside of that, you want to descend at a rapid rate, probably try and land somewhere soft as well.'

Looking along the coastline, Kirsten could see a beach. There was a road running beside it, but it was also far enough away from the main road, and she wondered if the beach could be seen. She read the grid coordinates over to Inspector Woodrow.

'That's a fairly remote beach, wildlife reserve around the side of it. Most people don't get to go in.'

'That'll be it then,' said Kirsten. 'They've dropped into there, where a van picked up Kirstie Macintyre, and off they go. Who knows where they are now?'

'It's still conjecture, though, isn't it?' said Woodrow. 'There's no proof.'

'We don't always wait for proof. Quite often, my work is done on the fly, trusting my gut, and seeing where it leads to. With the threat hanging over our two celebrities, I need to start making a move on this, but I'll continue to work in the shadows. Please, continue with your own thoughts. If we bring someone to justice, we're going to need all the evidence we can get.'

Kirsten felt an eerie silence as she got up, wondering if she'd been too forceful, taking the lead over the two police officers, but stuff that, she couldn't hang about. She had to sort things out and quickly.

Leaving the inspector's office, she found the police canteen and picked up her phone and called Justin Chivers.

'Justin, take down all of these coordinates.' Kirsten rhymed them off. 'First, the sighting for the parachute, and then the potential landing site at the beach. I want you to get onto CCTV of anything around there, anything at all. We're looking, potentially, for a van, something that's going to be picking up two parachutists and also a victim. See if we can find anything. It might be our only way to trace where Kirstie Macintyre has gone.'

'You think she's still alive?' said Justin.

'That's the theory. Two parachutes were seen coming out of the plane. Why blow her up? We've got the brochure and there's a specific time for this. They're not here to kill yet. They're here to kidnap. That's the way they want to work their terror. Let it build up in the media, using the very thing that gives these people, these celebrities, their oxygen, to turn it against them and hold up the horror. In some ways, it's quite clever.'

'Almost too clever for the average person that we get.'

'You're not wrong there, Justin. We heard from Dom and Carrie-Anne?'

'No, but they're on their way back. I expect I'll see them shortly.'

'Have you heard anything more on the internet, on the webs at all?'

'No,' said Justin. 'I was just about to speak to you about that. Everything seems to have gone quiet, very quiet. After all the talk of the big job and the big thing coming up, and we've had two major incidents, you'd expect there would be a lot of chatter, a lot of thought about what's going to happen, but nothing. It's like somebody got in there and silenced everybody. Put the fear of God into them.'

'I'm not sure it's God,' said Kirsten. 'Could be something worse. Did you receive the files from Anna, talking about the Huntress?'

'Yes, I have, and I'm keeping to my security protocols. Although I noticed you haven't, moonlighting on your own.'

'Boss's privilege,' said Kirsten. 'Besides, they'd be pretty brave to come into the police station and do anything.'

Kirsten closed down the call and after stopping in the canteen for a quick sandwich, she made her way out to the car park at the rear. She saw a car on the far side but looked over at where the murder team used to always park, the one she'd been on with Inspector Macleod. His car was there, and she fought the temptation to go up and have a word.

There was Hope's car beside Macleod's. Ross had his there too, a small, routine practical car, but then there was a little sports number. She stared at it, wondering just whose it was. She remembered that Macleod had taken on the woman from the art case, Clarissa Urquhart. Kirsten had met her briefly at a crime scene.

Kirsten was intrigued and walked over, staring at the car, admiring the lines of it without knowing if it was a quality car or not.

'Hands off,' said a voice behind her. She turned and saw Urquhart in a large shawl with tartan trousers. A brooch pinned the shawl across her and her hair looked fantastically purple.

'Sorry, I was just admiring it. I've not seen it here before.'

'Well, I've been here a while, love. Guess yours would have been here.'

'Yes,' said Kirsten. 'It used to be my spot you've got your car parked in.'

'Kirsten Stewart,' said the older woman. 'We met briefly that time.'

Kirsten stared at the woman. 'You're rather different to what I've expected. I was surprised when he took you on. No offense intended,' said Kirsten. 'It's just you didn't quite seem Macleod's type for the team.'

'Well, Seoras knows a good old bird when he sees one.'

Kirsten almost baulked at the comment. She couldn't see Macleod letting a comment like that go unchallenged.

'If you don't mind, I need to go. Nice to meet you again, Kirsten Stewart.' The woman stepped into the car, turned on the engine, quickly reversed, and spun around before driving out.

Clarissa Urquhart, thought Kirsten. *They said they needed someone like me, someone Macleod could relate to.* Kirsten turned around to step back to her car and felt that somebody was watching her. She looked up to see a face at the window. When she saw who it was, she gave a gentle wave. He might get annoyed at her for not popping in to see him, but she had things to do, and besides, with a target on her back, the last thing she wanted was go and talk to people she cared about. She climbed into her own car and began to drive the short distance back to her own office. She shook her head. Purple hair and a flash car. Macleod had changed.

Chapter 12

Orla Devlin waved away the makeup woman standing with a powder puff in her hand, trying to tap Orla's cheek. These people were always all over you, and it was the last thing she needed. *This is a wildlife programme. Who gives a stuff what the presenter looks like; the animals are the key thing.*

Besides, Orla didn't want to ruin her image. She was young, only twenty-seven, smart and intelligent, with a PhD in Zoology, but she'd finally hit the big time. One of the national programmes which toured around the country, looking at all the wildlife, and she, one of Scotland's own, was getting to present about the Cairngorms and the wildlife in it. Currently the snow line was high, but they'd gone up to be right where it changed, all the way up, just a short distance from the road.

She was to stand facing a road which in turn allowed a fantastic backdrop behind her. It would look like as if she were in the middle of nowhere, and yet, she was in one of the more accessible places. But she'd been sitting inside one of the Land Rovers, waiting for her cue to come out and perform.

They would be live, live across the nation, all the nations, in fact, right throughout the United Kingdom. Her face would be on television. She was well known in Scotland, because she had presented Scotland's own version of a nature watch for the last three years prior to that. She'd also been a model. It griped her that people thought she got this job simply because she looked good. With the makeup being plastered on her, she wanted to throw it all off and just be herself in front of the camera. Let people see that girl next door that she was.

Today she was going to talk to a mountain rescue expert who also was heavily into the local wildlife. Orla thought she probably knew more than this so-called local expert did, but that wasn't the point. She was there to ask the questions and look suitably amazed. She decided to wear a rather large jacket and reject the idea of the director that she should be standing there in jeans and a rather tight t-shirt. When she'd refused that, he talked about a jumper, but again, another one of those tight ones. She was here as an expert in Zoology, here as an expert about wildlife, here to educate the public. She'd done the years of marching along catwalks, or being in front of the camera, and being looked at and adored. Now, she wanted something real. Why couldn't people understand that?

'Orla, five minutes.'

She turned and nodded at the young lad who had run up to her. He seemed in awe of her, but he'd been very pleasant, fetching her whatever he thought she needed, when she'd been sitting in the Land Rover. She thought his name was Craig, could have been Johnny, though, or Jim, or James. He'd mumbled something at her when she'd asked. She hadn't had the time to turn around and ask him again, rather than make out that she didn't care. She simply called him star, which made the boy blush.

He was a boy, wasn't he? You could say that about somebody

who was nineteen. At twenty-seven, Orla was confused. Was she becoming a middle-aged woman or was she still one of the young ones? She also didn't know which she wanted to be. Middle-aged women on television were sometimes taken more seriously, she thought, if indeed women were taken seriously at all.

The show's director came forward with a man and introduced him to Orla. 'This is Jim Calhoun. Jim is the local expert; if you just hit the prompting notes there beside the camera, Orla, Jim will able to take care of all the detail.'

'I do actually know what we're talking about. I'm not just here to ask questions. I might go a little bit off the topic, if that's all right with you, Jim.'

The man nodded, but the director waved his hands in front of Orla, like she'd committed the worst offense in the world. 'I'm sorry, but no; you stick to the script, please.'

'You understand I know this stuff, don't you? You understand I can actually ask more pertinent and reasonable questions, not just the dribble you put up on a screen for me to recite.'

'Of course, we do, but we want you to be there as the face for the public. They're the ones who need the simpler questions, not yourself, and of course, we need to be able to see you smiling, beaming at them. You're that friendly image for the family. The one everybody likes. Now, you sure you want that jacket? We can go back down to the jumper or even the top if you want.'

Orla looked up at the director. 'I told you before, this is what I'm wearing. Look at it here, it's Baltic, man. It's absolutely Baltic.'

'I think she's right,' said Jim. 'I think she needs to be wearing that. That's what I'd be advising anybody up around here, to be well dressed. In fact, probably best if we can get a hat on. I know your hair's probably all right and keeping you warm. If people are out walking around here, especially in this weather, I'd advise that they put a hat on, like my own.' Jim tapped the hat on his head, but the director was shaking his own head furiously.

'No, we've just spent the last twenty minutes getting your hair right. We're not going to stick a hat on.'

'I've got a spare one if you haven't one?' said Jim, and pulled out a green and blue bobble hat. The director nearly fell over, having a canary, but Orla reached forward, took it off Jim, and put it on her head.

'Thank you,' she said. 'That's very thoughtful of you.'

'You are not wearing that.'

'I am,' said Orla, 'or I'll walk. We're going live in front of the country soon. I'll walk.'

The director backed down quickly. 'Okay, but smile, make sure you present yourself, and can we undo the jacket?'

'No,' said Orla 'we can't. Come here a minute, Jim.' She pulled Jim Calhoun away to one side. 'I'm sorry about him,' she said; 'what you're going to say is going to be important. I might go off topic a bit, push you on a few things, but it's just to get the information out. I hope that's all right with you. The key thing we want to do is obviously let people know about this place, know about the issues affecting it.'

'It's not a problem,' said Jim, 'you must find it hard.'

'Hard?' she said, 'In what way?'

'I used to see you, you know on those magazines. Nothing wrong with it, don't get me wrong, love. I thought you looked fantastic, and it's not like you were doing anything wrong. It was just bit of glamour. It's not that you showed anything or that, but it's hard for some people to distinguish it, isn't it? PhD in Zoology, you said?'

'Yes,' said Orla, 'I had to work hard for that, but it doesn't seem to count for much.'

'No, people see what they want to see,' said Jim. 'What I see is someone trying to make a difference, so you ask me what you want. Once we're live, I guess we can say, "Stuff him".'

'I just don't want you and me to be only a pretty picture. It's important you come across, well, Jim.'

'I'll be fine,' said Jim, 'don't worry about me; just you control that director of yours.' The man smiled, and Orla stuck a hand out, which at first caught Jim off guard, but then he shook it gently.

'Thank you,' said Orla. 'It's not often I get a sensible conversation like that.'

'Let's get in to set up the scene, get the lights on. Come on, now, people, let's move!' shouted the director.

Orla took Jim and repositioned him, standing with a glorious backdrop of a mountain behind her. The snow halfway up, the mountain turning from the usual brown and green layers to a crisp white.

'Thirty seconds, everyone,' shouted the director. Orla could see him almost panicking, turning this way and that, looking at everyone. 'Let's keep that lighting steady. Cameras, get ready to go. Counting in. We are five, four, three,' and then there was no noise, simply two fingers held up, then one, and then an arm telling Orla to go. In her earpiece, she could hear the voice of the national presenter.

'It's over to Orla Devlin, who's up in the Cairngorms. Wow, Orla. Looks pretty fresh up there.'

'Well, hello, Ian. Yes, it is fresh up here. We're right up on the snow line, and as you can see behind me, it's one heck of a view, but tonight I've got somebody very special with me, and I want to turn and talk to Jim Calhoun.'

As Orla turned, there wasn't a Jim Calhoun in front of her. Instead, a man in a balaclava was standing and she could hear the shock murmuring around the whole scene.

'Who the hell are you?' asked Orla. A gun was produced from the man's pocket and placed at Orla's head.

'Shut it. Just shut it. This is what you want on your television. This prettiness? Is this what you want to look at. For too long this world has been taken and run by people who are airheads, people who haven't got a clue, exploiting us, telling us what to think on television, but we've had enough. No more celebrities. In a new world order, everyone will have pride of place; everyone will be equal. You'll have your say, not these trumped-up people.'

Orla's face was a picture. Part of her was shaking, but another part of it was indignant of the comments that kept coming in from this man in a balaclava.

'I've got a PhD in Zoology. What the hell do you have?'

'He's got a gun,' shouted the director at Orla.

'I don't care if he's got a gun. Where did you go to school?'

The man turned and slapped Orla across the face, but she was undeterred. 'I mean it. You stand there with that gun and that, you tell me that 'Oh, she's an airhead celebrity. What have you got? I've got a PhD, you loser.'

The man reached up, clamped a hand across Orla's mouth, and pulled her close to him, the gun remaining at her head.

'We've had enough of the wild claims of these people, telling us they're intelligent, telling us this and that, telling us how to live lives. Well, we've decided it's time for an execution. The execution of *Celebrity*. In five days' time, these people will get their just desserts.'

Orla couldn't speak now, but she looked around and could see at least five more people with guns. The whole crew was under watch, no one was going to come to save her here. Jim Calhoun was sitting on the floor some distance away, his eyes watching her, gun pointed at him. The masked man started to drag Orla away and the director insisted the cameras follow him. She tried to kick and scream but the hand kept her mute, while her feet dug across the snow as she was dragged away. She saw Jim Calhoun get up, start to come towards her, but a gun was placed at his chest. She waved away his attentions, hoping that he would just sit back down again.

A van pulled up on the roadside, and the side door was flung open. As she was pushed towards the van, the man's hand slipped from her mouth and Orla Devlin shouted again, at the top of her voice, 'That's a PhD in Zoology! I wasn't just a model!'

Slowly the men with guns backed their way towards the van, getting in one by one, the weapons continuing to be trained on the small filming party. The cameraman kept coming forward and got the entire van in shot before it pulled off at breakneck speed.

'And cut,' said the director. 'Did we get all of that?'

'I think so.'

'What about her? What about Orla,' said Jim Calhoun, running over to the director.

'She was terrific, wasn't she? All that thing about a PhD in Zoology. That's going to go down well, isn't it? Quite funny in its own way.'

'No. What about her? She's just been grabbed.'

'Probably a stunt, though, isn't it? She's probably set it up herself.'

'No, she didn't,' said Calhoun. 'Have you not seen the papers recently? Where are you from?'

'London, come up to do the shoot. Why?'

Calhoun grabbed his mobile phone and started looking for signal. He didn't have any, and so he ran over to one of the Land Rovers. Getting inside, he found the keys and began driving down the hillside, until he realised that his phone had a bar of signal. Dialling 999, he asked for police, and told them about the kidnap of Orla Devlin.

It didn't take long before it had broken, having been broadcast on live national television. Kirsten watched from her own office as the incident happened, knowing she was too far away to make a difference. She would get to it, try and follow what was going on, but the police would be trying to launch a helicopter, get anything in the air to follow this van. As Kirsten watched the news come on with a special bulletin, she noted that they announced it as the former model being kidnapped. No one spoke of her wildlife endeavours, and certainly, nobody mentioned that she had a PhD in Zoology.

Chapter 13

K irsten stared at the screen in front of her, watching the massed ranks of newspaper reporters, all desperately concerned about their colleague Orla Devlin and pondering such platitudes that it almost made her sick. It was a circus being made out of her disappearance. Maybe that was the point. The woman was missing, in imminent danger, and all these people could do was turn the whole thing into some sort of sideshow.

Kirsten watched as they cut back to the studio where a presenter was in tears, but valiantly carrying on in front of the camera. They constantly talked about moments they had spent with Orla and how she was such a lovely person and her young children at home, photographs of which were paraded on the TV along with her smiling face. Her husband was in pieces, but the camera was still stuck in his face several times asking how he felt.

How the heck would you feel? thought Kirsten. *The man was in pieces trying to hold it together for some kids who were wondering where mom was. Yet, all that mattered was the camera kept rolling, kept putting this scene of misery up on the television.* 'After all, she was one of our own presenters,' they kept saying.

'If you keep watching that, you'll go insane,' said Justin Chivers. 'I always find it's better to get the reports rather than from off the telly.'

'Yes, but they've got a lot of people at the scene. I haven't so far,' said Kirsten. 'They've also just ramped it up, haven't they? Five days to execution. Five days to find them. That's three taken.'

'Will that be an end of it, though?' asked Justin. 'I think it might not be. They might go further.'

Kirsten spun on her heel. 'Then I need you to find me some links between these people, Kirstie Macintyre, Orla Devlin, Angus Argyle. I need to know what's the commonality here. Why them?'

'It could just be that they're in the public eye. At the end of the day, you don't get much bigger than Kirsty Macintyre. People who have seen Orla Devlin, either with animals or in a bikini, and anyone that's into radio, well, they'll know Angus Argyle, Hootsman and all that, but there may be more.'

'You'll need to come up with something then; otherwise, we're just going to have to guard every celebrity in the world, or at least in Scotland until their five days is up.'

'I'll get into it,' said Justin, 'but calm down. Anyway, I've gathered the others. You said you wanted to speak to us.'

'I'll be into the room in a minute. I just want to keep an eye on something here.'

'Very good,' said Justin, 'see you shortly.'

Kirsten looked back at the screen which was showing footage of Orla being taken. She watched how the gunmen came in, how quietly it was done. Everything was so calm, but very public. They could try to run voice recognition on those who spoke but Kirsten doubted anything substantial would come back from it. In the back of her mind, she wondered, *Could the Huntress be playing a game here?*' It seemed to be so busy out in the open, her hand being forced. *Is this what they want?*

She watched the movements of the kidnappers and once again, they looked practiced, at ease. They looked like they were for hire, not some sort of random lunatic group. Something was bugging Kirsten about all this, something was kicking at her and she knew from her time previously, working with Inspector Macleod, that if something gave you an itch, you had to find out what it was because it would never leave, not until it was uncovered.

Having satisfied her curiosity, Kirsten marched into the conference room where Dom, Carrie-Anne, and Justin were sitting, eyes eagerly looking up at her as she entered.

'Anything further on the kidnapping?' said Dom.

'No,' said Kirsten. 'That's not why I called you in. Right, I've been speaking to Anna and it appears that we have some people after us.'

'Like we didn't know that,' said Dom.

'Easy,' said Carrie-Anne, 'easy.'

'Now, I know who it is. We call her the Huntress. Over there, she's called Охотница.'

Carrie-Anne's face was blank, but Dom's eyes narrowed. 'She's after us? I thought she was just a rumour. She's never been sighted, has she?'

'No, but I think it's to do with Control. Craig killed Control and we believe that the Huntress may have been tied into her. This looks like revenge. That's why they're coming for us.'

'You want to stick her in the ground?' said Dom. 'You want us to hand this investigation over, I take it. We'll go hide until a clean-up crew can sort them out.'

'No,' said Kirsten, 'We aren't going anywhere. We aren't putting off what we do for somebody else coming after us.'

'It's the smart move,' said Dom. 'Get somebody good in to peel them off our back. Stay hidden until then.'

'We've got five days until some celebrities are going to be killed and it's our job to stop that. The fact we have somebody coming after us for stopping them previously is neither here nor there. We'll continue to operate in pairs. We'll be careful and watch how we go, but whatever happens, we are not being put off what we do.'

'Did Anna say we should continue?'

Kirsten ignored the comment. 'I'd offer to get another team in, but this is our mess, specifically my mess. I'm going to clean that up. Anna is, however, on the case as well.'

'Let's hope she acts quickly then,' said Dom. 'I don't like the idea of running around with a target on my back. If it hadn't been for Carrie-Anne, I'd have been long gone by now.'

'It wasn't Carrie-Anne. It was you. The pair of you playing it sensibly, understanding there was also something else in play, and that's what we do. Justin, I don't want you out unless you have to be. Stay here in the offices. I'll warn downstairs to be on the lookout as well. Nobody comes up here without express permission from us. Even if they're part of the service. Nobody comes up here. The team only. That's it.'

'Did Anna say anything about how long the woman was going to be here? How much effort she would put into coming after us?' asked Dom.

'Anna's still working on it, but our movements were being tracked. Somebody inside the organisation knew something. Anna's gone after them.'

Dom stood up from his chair and started to pace around behind the table. 'I'm not comfortable with this. Easier to disappear. Somebody else can take care of these celebrities. Somebody else can get in there. We're not the only ones who can prevent tragedies, not the only ones who can do this job,' said Dom.

'No, we're not,' said Kirsten. 'Did you forget where I was brought up? Spent all my younger days in a mixed martial arts ring. When they come for you in there, you don't hide. You come back at them. If we hide and somebody else comes in and starts to sort the problem, the next one will come again, and we'll hide again. They don't know us. They think they can just come after us, tit for tat. If someone comes after us, I want them to understand what they are doing. I want them to understand that it's them or us. We won't pussyfoot around them. We'll bury them.'

'You don't mean that,' said Dom. 'What you mean is, we'll capture them, we'll stick them to the service, and we'll put them away in a room somewhere or a prison, and then they'll get traded back, and then the circle will come again. You don't have it in you to finish something off like this,' said Dom.

'Don't speak to me like that,' raged Kirsten.

'Well, you don't. Don't get me wrong. If it's there in the moment, they are going to kill you or kill somebody else, you will fire. You will shoot back, but if you catch them, you won't eliminate them. You'll hand them over to see what information you can get out.'

'Well, I won't kill people in cold blood, but we'll wake them up.'

'What Dom means,' said Carrie-Anne, 'is you can't do that. They'll always come back. They'll always get traded. You see, somebody else will see an angle. Somebody else will see something they need, and these people, these people will have their revenge on you. These people who have this grudge on you, they won't sit back. Once they're traded, they'll come again, and this time you might not even see them coming because you might not know they've been traded. We have an advantage at the moment in that at least we know they're coming. We know to hide.'

'Exactly,' said Dom.

'Well, I'm with the boss,' said Justin, 'you can't let them see that you're afraid.'

'What do you know about it?' said Dom. 'You're not a field agent. How often do you get your hands dirty out there? You won't be the one that's exposed. You'll be sat up here, safe and away from it all, while there's a target on my back.'

'That's enough, Dom. Justin is a target as well; you know that,' said Kirsten.

'Do I?' said Dom. 'Do I really? Carrie-Anne and I will be the ones out there. Sure, you will too, but we're the ones running the dirty work on this investigation.'

'I am not putting down what we were assigned to do,' said Kirsten. 'Five days to go. We're close. We don't bring another team in.'

'What about Craig?' asked Dom. 'Where's he in all this? He's not exactly running around with that target on his back with us.'

'Craig's gone into hiding,' said Kirsten. 'He doesn't have a team to back him up the way we do.'

'Anna would have told him. Anna will want us to do the same, won't she?'

'Anna wants us to run away and hide,' said Kirsten, 'while

she sorts it all out, but that's not me. If you want to, you can go into hiding, Dom. You too, Carrie-Anne. I'll get a couple of new bodies in. They won't be the same. I won't know how to trust them so I may just have to run this on my own with Justin.'

'I won't leave you like that,' said Carrie-Anne. 'We either all go, or we all stay and carry on. We're not here to split the team. We'll be safer together.'

'She's right about that,' said Dom, 'but we'll be safer in hiding together.'

'No,' said Kirsten. 'We're better out there finding them because they'll come.'

'If they come, we need to put them down,' said Dom. 'Understand that, okay? You need to get that into your head. This isn't like a lot of what you've done. Yes, I know you could have been killed before, but this is something where you have to finish it. You have to call an end to it, not simply arrest them. Not a superhero exercise where we keep sticking them back in the asylum. No, this, if it's a vendetta, has to be finished. I'll stay out if you want to, but you tell me you can end it. You tell me that we can clear up after this. We can dispose of the loose ends, not simply pack them away somewhere.'

Kirsten stared at Dom, part of her reeling. During all this spy business, she knew she had to kill. It was so different from being a policewoman, but even when she killed, she killed in self-defence. The people weren't vulnerable at the time. They were trying to kill her or somebody else. She was trying to protect. Dom was asking her to put somebody down no matter what to save her own hide in the future, to send a message. *He is right*, thought Kirsten. *He knows what he's all about, but inside, I don't know if I could truly do it.* But with the team about to fracture around her, Kirsten did the only thing she knew she had to do.

'Trust me, I'll do it,' she said. Dom stared at her for a number of seconds before turning away.

'Okay, let's get on with it then. Let's get on with finding these celebrities. What's our next move?'

'Next move is Justin's. He needs to come up with something. Needs to get a link. Until then, stay off the streets. Get into the files and phone the TV company. See if you can get anybody talking about how she could have been grabbed. How did they just walk in? See if you can get onto voice recognition. These people who did the kidnapping, they didn't look like amateurs. They looked more professional than that. They looked like people who knew what they were doing. It was all quick, quite easy. I don't think these celebrities are simply all part of a random grab. It's been thought out. Why these ones?'

'They'll be a link,' said Kirsten. 'They'll be something that ties them. Something to justify this beyond they're just a celebrity. Whoever is doing it is trying to teach the public a lesson about something. We're not seeing it. Kill people because they're celebrities. Well, it's false because it's a trumped-up thing, but you look at them. Poor Devlin, she's just a reporter. A good-looking woman at that. Some people may think she got there at the expense of other people's talent, but at the end of the day, she's just a reporter. Then a DJ, why take a DJ? Most people didn't recognise him, except they recognised the voice. Why make a public example of him? Let's check, does he fundraise for anybody? Does he have anything controversial in his background?'

'Nothing's come forward so far,' said Justin. 'I'll try and cross-reference though. Maybe they could grab a few more, make it

110

easier.'

Kirsten rolled her eyes over at Justin. 'I don't care what it is, you find it. Find me that link because if you do, we might find who else is going to get kidnapped before they dispose of him. We might be able to get on the front foot and capture them before they can go through with this.'

'We will do, boss,' said Dom, 'but watch that target on your back. You better have eyes on the back of your head because I bet you haven't been hunted before. I have, and it's not pretty.'

Chapter 14

Anna Hunt walked along the stony grey path through the London park that she knew well. She was heading for one corner of it, one that generally wasn't sought after by most of the London public. A particular area with a large clump of trees and a bench deep amongst them. Often when she wanted to think, she would take that path, sit there knowing that she wouldn't be disturbed, not even by dog walkers passing through, for that particular area even smelled slightly due to a badly placed sewer not far away.

It wasn't the smell that Anna went for; it was the solitude, the chance in the busy space of London to find somewhere without people. Anna was an operator through and through, but she liked times to reflect and think though she was a woman who could act and act quickly. Her mind was always active, looking at the different angles of the situation, working out the possible outcomes and how to adopt them, manipulate them, and come out with what was the best solution either for her or her Service or whatever needed to be done.

The air was crisp and chilly, but the sun was shining as she walked along, seeing the everyday Londoner out and about. There was a man running along the lake with shorts that really didn't suit him. He smiled as he passed a woman running the other way and Anna imagined he'd simply come out in them to meet her. Beyond him was the dog walker, the dog on the lead, one of those extendable ones, although it was so loose she wondered what was the point of it.

She'd often thought of having a dog, but she was away too often. She thought about the companionship, someone who she could lavish affection on without worrying about if she would be betrayed, without worrying that the animal needed more from her than she could give, but a dog wouldn't work. After all, Anna was away so often and the dog needed some sort of stability, a home life. It needed someone it could run up to when they came through the door every day, a lap of its owner to sit on as they read a book or watched television or sat by the fire. Someone to take it out for walks. No, Anna needed to be alone in life. She had put distance between herself and her sister, and that had nearly gone wrong. Until she was clear of this life in the Service, Anna wouldn't have anyone . . . or anything too close.

She followed the path as it bent off, and she could smell the slight stench of sewage as she headed towards the dark copse of trees. Rounding the largest one, she saw a man sitting on the bench, smart black trousers, black shoes, but with a brown leather jacket. It was one of the longer ones that reached down past his hips and certainly only worn by an older gentleman. He had a hat on his head, brown as well, with a darker brown band around it. As she crunched away along the path, he looked up without a smile. Beyond the bench was a small path out through the back of the trees and Anna could see the road beyond. The path out to it bent slightly, so anyone coming in would have to get fully inside the copse before they could see anyone, but you could see the glimpses of traffic through the trees.

'They say this is where you come often. It's hardly the most deliberate space. I'm not sure I could meditate with that sort of smell around my nostrils.'

'You get used to it,' said Anna and sat down beside Godfrey. 'How have things been going?' she asked.

'Well, after a little bit of digging, all the signs add up. I haven't got proof, so we're not going to be able to take her in, and if she leaves now once she meets you, all hell could be there to pay, so whatever you're going to do, make sure it's tidied up.'

'I always tidy up my own area; you know that.' Anna turned and looked at Godfrey who gave her a faint smile.

'How is our lady up in the north?' asked Godfrey.

'She took it okay, but she insists on continuing to work.'

'That doesn't sound very wise. Is she a martyr?'

'No, she's a copper behind it.'

'Well, she needs to become a spy or she won't last,' said Godfrey.

'She's good with me. I can provide the backbone. She'll grow one eventually.'

'Sometimes this job isn't kind to you,' said Godfrey. 'Sometimes you have to do things that you really dislike, but she has to develop a coldness. She seems to have a warmth towards her team.'

'There's nothing wrong with her warmth. I have a warmth for her.'

Godfrey turned and stared at Anna before his lip bent downwards and he gave a shrug of her shoulders. 'Maybe you do,' he said, 'but I never questioned your efficiency. You're always prepared to do what it takes. Is she that way as well?'

'She goes beyond what it takes at times. She sees a world there to be put right, things to be corrected, and this trouble that's visiting her, it came from her saving you. We owe her,' said Anna.

'You don't owe anyone in this game,' said Godfrey. 'You're going soft.'

'No, but you have to build your alliances. You have to build people you can rely on, people you can trust. Look at us; it took time for us to get to this point, but you trusted me. I cleared out some of your bad eggs.'

'I'm bringing you yours,' said Godfrey. 'She's called Juliet. She'll be coming through in a couple of minutes. Like I say, whatever you have to do, make sure you clean it up.'

'Will the car be at my disposal?'

'Depends how long you are. Give it at least ten minutes, I need to be dropped off. After that, yes, it'll be at your disposal.'

Godfrey reached inside his jacket and picked up his phone. He made a call and simply said one word, 'Nay.' He put the phone back inside his jacket and turned to Anna. 'Be very careful. The Huntress, she's quite formidable, they say. She has not operated much in this part of the world before, but where she has been, she's brutal, lethal, and, by the sounds of it, she's hungry for it.'

'Cold and detached, that's what you just said to me, wasn't it? No sentiment here.' Anna smiled as Godfrey stood up.

'Best of luck.'

He turned around and walked across from the bench, making his way out to the road. Anna watched him and saw someone pass him on the path. The woman stood only five-feet two high. She had long brown hair and was dressed in a long skirt with a blue jumper on top of it. A leather jacket hung off her shoulders but hadn't been put on, giving the impression that there was actually warmth in the air, something Anna did not find to be true. As Juliet walked closer, Anna stood up from the bench, and stared the woman up and down.

'You're Juliet?' she said, and the woman nodded. Anna moved to the end of the bench towards the woman who was looking quizzically at her. 'You're wondering who I am. My name is Anna Hunt.'

The woman turned to run, but Anna had a hand on her wrist, grabbing it tight. With her other hand, she reached up and grabbed the woman's neck, swiftly moving her towards the bench, and sitting her down. The woman scrabbled with her hands trying to get Anna off her, but Anna pinned her to the bench with one forearm, and from her jacket pocket, took out a needle and stabbed it in her neck.

'Sit still,' said Anna, 'sit still and don't move. You have five minutes to live. If you want the antidote, you'll start to speak.' The woman glared at her but shook her head.

'The Huntress, you've been in contact, haven't you?'

The woman shook her head. Anna started to count in her head, thirty seconds, not yet time.

'I know the Huntress is after some of my people. I want to know what she looks like. I want to know where she's operating. How did you speak to her? How did you pass on what was happening?'

The woman was silent.

'I know where you work in the organisation. Godfrey told me. Godfrey thinks it's you. Of course, we don't have time for a tribunal over that; we don't have time to pull you out and to say, 'This one's been lying, throw her in a cell.' You'll speak to me if you want to live.'

Anna went quiet and the woman simply looked at her, saying nothing. Beyond the copse, Anna could hear a dog bark. There were birds up in the trees, but again, the woman remained silent. Three minutes passed.

'You have less than two minutes left, you're going to find your breathing starts to go first.' As if on cue, the woman started to wheeze. 'I can help you with that,' said Anna; 'really, I can, but you're not giving me anything, any reason.'

'She's in the UK,' said the woman breathlessly. 'She's operating. I – I never-never saw her. She's – she's, uh, sister, the sister of Control. She's – she's here for Kirsten Stewart and that man of hers, Craig. They want them; that's who they want for killing Control. She wants to take as many as possible with her; she doesn't care. Take out the organisation, take you out too if she knew who you were.'

'And Godfrey?'

'Too big for her target. She needs to make sure. It's her first time in the UK.'

'What did you get for it?'

'Give me the antidote. I need the antidote.' The woman's breathing got tighter. 'What did you get for it?' asked Anna.

'Money,' said the woman, 'a lot of money.'

Anna leaned back. If the woman had said her family had been taken and tortured, she'd have felt for her. If the woman had said there'd been threats against her, she'd have felt for her, but money, to betray everyone for money. How much money made that all worthwhile? How much money made that okay?

'You think – it will make – a difference? Why not – money? We work – like slaves, we put – ourselves at risk for – this country – for what? What sort of – pension do you have? Not much, – is it? I gave up – a boyfriend. He died – a field

117

operative, and he died – for what?'

Anna stood up and looked down at the woman raving on the bench now, her breathing becoming sharp. *Thirty seconds tops*, thought Anna, *that's all she's got.* She reached inside her jacket, and took out a small vial. 'This is your antidote.' The woman went to reach up with her hands but found that she couldn't.

'Give me – give me – antidote, inject me – inject me.'

Fifteen seconds, thought Anna. *She's going to know, know what I think.* Anna threw the vial on the ground and crunched it under her foot. 'Like hell. You sell my team out for money? Just money, like hell.'

Anna stood and watched the woman as she breathed her last, and then quickly put her arms together. For a woman who looked small, Anna Hunt was deceptively strong and she rolled the woman over onto her front so she hung over Anna's shoulder.

Slowly, she walked to the path at the rear of the copse of trees. It took twenty seconds before the car passed and she had her hand up. The driver, on seeing her, turned the car around, and pulled up alongside the pavement. Anna quickly opened the rear door and put the woman inside. 'Send Godfrey my apologies,' said Anna, 'but this one didn't make it. It was her, though.'

'Is there anything else I need to take care of?' asked the driver.

'No. Money, it was just money.'

Chapter 15

Kirsten hung up the phone and made her way over to the window of her office. She scanned the street, but there was nothing suspicious down there. She wasn't worried about anyone taking a pot shot up at the window for the glass was bulletproof, but the news that had come from Anna Hunt was disturbing. There had been an inside mole and the actions of her team had been followed.

They operated independently to a point, but details of who they were, where they lived, were all out there in the open. Kirsten was putting a mandatory *Stay at the office*, on all of them. Unless they were out on field operations, they'd be staying in this building in the camp beds downstairs until they'd sorted these things out. Someone else could go round, check on their premises, make sure their homes were okay.

Kirsten drank a large coffee as she stood looking out of the window. Downstairs could be seen popping out occasionally, making sure the street was clear. Kirsten wondered if anyone realised that the little old lady had a handgun with a stopping power of almost a small truck inside it. *It's funny*, thought Kirsten, *she would shoot to kill*, even though she had no idea of who this was coming after Kirsten, even though she had no idea what sort of trouble Kirsten was in and why.

The service was strange. After working in the police where there were so many rules and regulations, the things she was getting involved in now seemed so very different. She almost wanted a good chat about it, wanted to sit down with Macleod and talk to him. Maybe her former inspector could shed thoughts on it. How could she keep herself as herself without giving way to the need to kill, even when not being shot at? Dom was right. If this threat wasn't taken out properly, it could come back to haunt them for years to come. At least now they knew it was coming; in the future, who knew?

There came a knock on the door and it swung open. Kirsten didn't turn around. She could tell by the type of rap, it was Justin coming into the room.

'Boss, I've got something.'

Kirsten spun around. 'What?'

'Come in the office. I can show you on the computer easier.'

Kirsten made her way out of the office and followed Justin across to his, where she watched him slide in behind a large bank of computer screens. She joined him behind his chair as he pointed up to the leftmost screen.

'Okay, so far, if you take a look, you've got Angus Argyll; you've also got Kirstie Macintyre and then there's Orla Devlin. It's taken a while, but I think I can find what's behind it. The three of them don't tend to link very well. I can't see Kirstie Macintyre being upstaged by somebody like Orla. Orla's a bit younger than her. I think on the same screen, she might show her up, but they did all attend a fundraiser.'

'What sort of fundraiser?' asked Kirsten.

'It was for an orphanage. I don't know why this makes them targets, but it's the only thing I can find with the three of them.

There were five Scottish celebrities. They all pledged their support behind this. When you look at it, it was actually quite big; there was television with it.'

'So why has it taken you so long to pick it up?'

'I wasn't looking for that, was I? I was checking families, where they live, what business connections they had. This was different. This was just a charity fundraiser, sitting, staring me in the face but it's the only thing I can come up with.'

'So, is there anybody else involved in those fundraisers?'

'Well, there's two other celebrities. There's Donald Hassim; he's that media tycoon, bit of a showman on the telly, always talking about business. Apparently, his mother was Scottish, but his father isn't, but he's always appearing and telling people how to use their money, what to do with it. Seen as a sound voice for advice and that, and he's quite glitzy with it as well; seems to always like to be on the telly.'

'And who's the next one?'

'Kelly Haig.'

'The model? A magazine celebrity?' said Kirsten.

'Exactly, Kelly Haig, in her thirties now, but not that long from exhibiting her body.'

'It's a bit of a mix though, isn't it? I mean Kelly Haig used to show all and sundry, all the magazines and that. Then you've got a businessman. You've got a DJ that's quite popular amongst families and that; Orla Devlin, a good and upcoming star, but she's no way related to anything like Kelly Haig is. Then you've got Kirstie Macintyre. You'd almost say she's above them all, a big celebrity.'

'And yet this is the one thing that ties the first three together. That's the only thing we've got, boss. I'm suggesting we put some protection around these other two, at least until we can find a better lead.'

'I think you're right. I'm going to go and have a word with the chief constable. We've got a problem; we can't protect them both. We haven't got the numbers, the way they're going in and grabbing people. I'd want at least our team with one of them, get protection up for the other.'

Kirsten left the room, made her way back to her office and picked up the phone.

'It's Anna here. What's the matter?'

Kirsten relayed the information she'd found out. 'I'd like to get another team from the service up. I can't protect both these celebrities with my own team. Best we bring a second, separate group in.'

'No,' said Anna, 'with the threat on you, I'm not bringing another team into that. If you let the police guard them, the Huntress won't come after them. There's no point, there's no Service involvement. She'll not be interested. She will only come after Service. It's what we do in this world we work in; you don't involve the local police force.'

Kirsten had to agree that Anna was right, best to keep people out of this as best she could; it would be a good idea.

'Okay,' said Kirsten, 'I'll talk to the chief constable, give him whole charge of one of them and we'll take the other.'

'I would suggest that you take the ex-model as I feel Mr Hassim will probably have his own security around him as well. Best if the police supplement that. I doubt Kelly has any.'

'Will do,' said Kirsten and put the phone down again before phoning the chief constable. As she outlined why she thought Donald Hassim was at risk, she could hear the bemusement in the chief constable's voice.

'It's not very conclusive, is it?'

'No,' said Kirsten, 'but it's the only thing we've got. There's nothing else linking any other celebrity, and we've only got a few days. If we can interrupt their plans in any way, even if it is on a hunch, well then, best we try it.'

'We're not getting further forward on our own end with only a few days left. It's not going to cost that much to provide the protection either. We'll do it.'

Kirsten thanked the man and then decided how best she wanted to approach this. She called the team for a meeting five minutes later, sitting them down in front of the large round table in the conference room.

After explaining the detail of how they'd found out about the other two celebrities, and her conversation with the chief constable, Kirsten decided to ask her team for suggestions about how to go about protecting Kelly Haig.

'I'd put one person directly on her. Someone to stay tight to her.'

'Oh, aye,' said Carrie-Anne, 'and I bet you'll be the one to do that.'

Dom gave a little grin. 'It doesn't really matter, does it? I think she's a bit too young for me, but the premise is sensible so I'm going to go everywhere with her to see the options for protection. The rest of us at a distance. If we can pick out where she wants to be when she's going on her appointments, the others can scan there first.'

'We haven't got a lot of us and one thing I'm not happy about is having one person in the open in front of her, with us being targets that can make her target of not just these kidnappers, but of the Huntress as well. You could lose Kelly in the crossfire. I don't agree, Dom,' said Kirsten.

'She's right,' said Carrie-Anne, 'we can't take the risk of that.

We'll have to operate around her. In fact, I think the best thing to do is not even tell her we're there.'

'What? Provide cover while keeping in the dark ourselves?' queried Dom

'Absolutely,' said Kirsten, 'if we're not seen around her and we operate in the dark, then less likely we're going to get picked up and seen. I know what you're saying, Dom, but for the protection of our own team, I think we need to stay dark on this one.'

'Why don't we just get somebody else in then?' said Dom. 'Why don't we go to ground?'

'Because Anna's on the hunt. We're going to flush out this Huntress. We're going to meet her head on. That's why,' said Kirsten; 'that's why we're doing it. We can't take this sort of nonsense. You can't take this from someone. You can't run and hide. You have to stand up and beat them down and let it be seen by everybody else.'

Dom turned away in his chair.

'Don't turn your back on me,' said Kirsten.

'Well, I've said my piece and I'll do my job but what we're doing is compromising everybody here. This is not sensible. I don't like this.'

Kirsten shot a glance at Carrie-Anne.

'Well, it's an option, isn't it? There's no good solution here. If we go to ground, boss, you're right, we could end up just making a rod for our backs for years to come. If we stand up and face it, we'll lay down our marker for other people as well. It's your call, you're the boss, what you're both saying has merit.'

'Then the call is made,' said Kirsten, 'we face up to this. Dom, Carrie-Anne, I want you to go and check out Kelly's security.

See what she has and be careful out there, you never know who's watching us so do it on the quiet, make sure she doesn't see you, but let us understand what protection she needs then.'

'Are you going to keep a full time watch on her?' asked Carrie-Anne.

'We'll need to, but let's see what support she's got to begin with.'

Carrie-Anne stood up and put on her coat before returning to Dom. 'Come on, you heard the boss.'

Dom rose up, turned around, and made his way over to Kirsten. 'I don't like it,' he said, 'Trust me, I don't like it. We'll go, we'll get it done but we've cut it fine—too fine, already.' With that, he left the room, leaving Carrie-Anne staring at Kirsten.

'He's right,' she said, 'he has a point.'

'Go check on Kelly Haig for me,' said Kirsten. 'Give me a shout when you've done that.'

The room went silent. Kirsten looked at the table in front of her. She almost wanted a piece of paper to look at, to pick up and pretend she was reading because she knew Justin was looking at her.

'Anna got those moments; you're going to get them, too. You're in charge, you're the boss and they're not always going to like it, and some of your decisions are actually going to be wrong, so just make them and get on with it,' said Justin. 'Dom always goes cautious. He operates in the dark and now he's not as strong as he used to be. Maybe not as fast as he used to be but his brain still works as quick, but he would like to operate without being seen. To take the advantage from there. That's why he doesn't like it. Putting them out like that, he doesn't think he's up to it anymore.'

'Do you think he's right with that?' asked Kirsten.

'He's slower than he used to be. He did ask or mentioned about getting out recently. I think Dom's thinking about moving on. This business takes it out of you. I know that, and I work behind a desk. The constant looking over your shoulder and a constant need to prevent yourself from being surveyed. The constant requirement of being alone, detached from people, it's not easy.'

'Do you think he needs that?'

'I think he wants it,' said Justin, 'it's not just a need. Dom's given a lot in his life to this service. Now he wants to go.'

'Well, why hasn't he gone then? Nobody's stopping him,' said Kirsten. 'He's free to leave and put his notice in.'

'Dom has been in this service and all his friends are here. At least those we do call friends. He won't leave while she's here.'

'Who?' asked Kirsten. 'Carrie-Anne? Are they . . . ?'

'No,' said Justin, 'it hasn't got that far but it's going to. He wants to go but he wants to go with her. He's worried that if he goes on his own, he'll be on his own. I don't have that. I have my man at home. I can go when I'm ready. I'll just miss the excitement and obviously the quality coffee.'

Kirsten gave a laugh but at the back of her mind was brewing the thought about Dom and Carrie-Anne.

'They're both alone, aren't they? Probably best if they go together.'

'That's not your choice or yours to engineer,' said Justin, 'if you don't mind me saying so, boss. But we're out in the open here and if Carrie-Anne goes down because we didn't run and hide, I don't think Dom will forgive you.'

Kirsten placed her elbows on the table and put her head in her hands.

'You don't have to feel guilty about it; it's his choice and hers.'

'Except it was mine to put us out there. I hope we don't lose her either because I don't know if I'd recover from it.'

Chapter 16

Kirsten stood in the changing cubicle and quickly stripped off before digging out a black swimsuit. She put her hair up in a swimming cap, listening to the snap of it as she pulled it tight down over her head. Stepping out of her own cubicle, she looked around to see if anyone was watching. The ladies' changing rooms of the spa on the edge of Inverness were fairly deserted, but she had tailed Kelly Haig to here and was now about to enter the spa area where her protectee would, no doubt, be enjoying herself, taking a relaxing break from her daily grind.

Kirsten had been forced to buy a swimsuit and, in fairness, it fitted reasonably well. The swim cap had been an afterthought, helping to disguise her hair. She wasn't worried about Kelly Haig spotting her; rather, she had one eye out on the general public just in case one of them turned out to be from the Huntress.

Kirsten made her way into a steam room where she sat down in the seat opposite Kelly Haig. The woman had long blonde hair with highlights in it, and the sweat was running down off her shoulders onto what Kirsten had to admit was still a good-looking body. The woman had given up appearing with even less clothes on in magazines and now appeared most of the times in celebrity magazines wearing a lot more and talking about her lovely home.

With all that, she still had her figure, but Kirsten could tell the difference between someone who simply tried to keep it in shape and someone who could carry out cardiac exercises without batting an eyelid. Kirsten was the latter; Kelly Haig, the former. Also, inside the steam room was an older man in dark trunks. Kirsten kept casting her eye towards him, but he rarely looked at Kirsten, his eyes darting over to Kelly most of the time. However, the steam seemed to get to him and he left the room, leaving the two women alone.

'You're Kelly Haig, aren't you?' asked Kirsten.

The woman smiled, 'Yes, that's me.'

'I recognised you from the magazines. Do you come here often? It's my first time,' said Kirsten.

'I try and come when it's quiet, especially when you get men like that. Sometimes I just want time to myself.'

'I get that,' said Kirsten. 'I really do, but are you not a bit worried at the moment?'

'Worried? Why would I be worried?' asked Kelly.

'Other celebrities being taken. They took that Kirstie Macintyre, didn't they? Blew her up in that plane? A DJ was kidnapped and then that Orla was carried off. I mean that Orla was quite good looking, wasn't she? Maybe they'll be after somebody like you as well.' Kelly Haig looked a little bit disturbed.

'Oh, sorry,' said Kirsten, 'I didn't mean to sort of agitate you. I was just surprised that you were out and about so openly.'

'They're not going to want me, are they?' said Kelly.

'I thought you'd have security or something, some big

strapping lad watching the door and that. That'd be quite good,' said Kirsten. 'I like a man with a bit of muscle.'

'No, no. I don't need it. I don't need any protection. I've never had anybody threaten me.'

Kirsten stood up and made her way across and sat down beside Kelly. The woman seemed happy enough with this arrangement. Kirsten felt the sweat pour from her head. She wasn't a big fan of steam rooms, and she certainly didn't think she could stay in here more than another five minutes or so.

'In case you're having any trouble, might be worth hiring us, just to look out for you.'

'I don't need to be silly,' say Kelly. 'Everybody loves me. I mean what have I done in my life except show my wobbly bits? People don't come and take you away for that. That DJ, he was always mouthing off, wasn't he? Same with that Kirstie Macintyre. She always had an opinion on the telly, and Orla Devlin, well, she's known for being a journalist and that. I'm not. What am I? I'm nothing. I tell people that my kitchen looks nice. I let them see around my home. I don't have a go at anybody. I can't see any man coming after me just because I look good. He's not going to execute me, is he? Not the sort of thing I'm in danger of.'

'I think it'd be wise to listen to us. Wise to just protect yourself. We're quite affordable,' said Kirsten.

'No,' said Kelly, standing up. 'Thanks, but no.'

Kirsten watched her leave the steam room. She had that walk, the wiggle of the hips, something that Kirsten never quite managed. Kirsten was a fighter. She wasn't there to look good; she was there to be good, there to be effective. Yes, she thought she had a figure worth considering but she didn't strut like a peacock the way Kelly had out of that steam room. There wasn't even anybody there to look except Kirsten. Maybe it was second nature to her.

Anyway, it seemed that she had no private protection anyway, so something learned. Kirsten waited a few minutes before making her way out of the steam room, and after going under the shower for five minutes, made her way back to her cubicle and dressed again. She picked up her phone and texted Dom giving him the go.

* * *

'So, she hasn't got any security, at least not a security team.'

'That's right; that's what the boss said,' said Dom, sitting beside Carrie-Anne in the car. 'I'll just go in and see if she's got anything that's worthwhile in the house.'

'Be careful.'

'And you,' said Dom. 'You're the one exposed out here.'

'I know what I'm doing,' said Carrie-Anne. 'Get in, have a look, get out.'

Dom nodded and exited the car, making his way slowly across the street. It was one of the posher ends of Inverness and the house had a large number of trees around it, sheltering the property from people looking in from the outside. Dom glanced up and down the street, saw no one in particular, and quickly jumped over the wall that ran around the property. It was only waist high, but he had to crawl in under the trees before appearing on a large immaculate lawn. There was large chess set and when he touched it, he realised it was plastic, not marble, and was slightly less impressed.

Kelly Haig plays chess out on the lawn. Surely that's got to be for the photoshoot. Dom stole around the edge of the house, looked up and saw the alarm system. He traced the wiring along and saw where it would run off to alert an outside company. He took a small device from his pocket, and quickly broke into the wires, bypassing that which would set off the alert and then made his way over to the rear door. Taking a set of keys, he unlocked it and marched in, stopping briefly, listening for an alarm, but none came. He had seen the speaker which would've blared out to all the neighbours, and he could also see that he was being detected on several interior systems but the alarm that would go out was not being activated.

Quickly, Dom made his way along a lavish hall, stopping momentarily to see a large picture of Kelly Haig in a rather skimpy bikini. *Bizarre to have it up on the wall*, he thought, and then made his way into the front room where, over the fireplace, was another large portrait of her in a sweeping ballgown that left little to the imagination.

She really loves herself, thought Dom. He began to rifle through the drawers that were in the room but found nothing of use. He made his way through several bedrooms, catching himself several times, as first he saw a waterbed, then a room with a mirror above it, and finally, a rather mundane bed which seemed to have been slept in recently. The covers were lying off and this was clearly what Kelly liked to use. Maybe the other bedrooms were for show; maybe they were for entertainment.

Dom ignored the thought, made his way over to the drawers of the room, but found only clothing and a large walk-in boudoir. He found plenty of makeup, even wigs, but there was nothing with which she could protect herself.

Dom went through the upstairs with a fine-tooth comb before he found it behind another portrait of Kelly, again one which left little to the imagination. Dom worked out the combination for the safe by taking a small device, placing it up on the safe, and slowly turning the clicker round and round. It took three goes, but the device came up with the combination that allowed Dom to open up the safe and find a handgun inside. He took the weapon out and turned it over in his hands. From the weight he reckoned there was no ammunition in it. He slid the magazine out and confirmed there were no bullets. He noticed the packet at the rear of the safe, but then he looked up inside the gun itself and realised that it was unlikely to fire because it hadn't been looked after. He wondered how long the woman had had this, and he doubted she would even be able to use it, if she could even fire the thing herself.

Dom made his way around the rest of the house but found little with which Kelly Haig could defend herself from and, and also realised he had got in so easily. Any professional worth their salt would follow without hesitation. *In fact*, he thought, *if they kicked in the door and grabbed her, by the time the alarm had got to an outside company, they'd be gone with her.*

It seemed to him that the only thing that was going to stop any assailant were the pictures on the wall, for they certainly caught your eye. Once you got over the initial look, Dom felt a narcissism about the woman that was frankly off-putting.

Dom retreated out of the house after locking up the safe, re-arranging everything back to where it was, and then returned for the wiring setup he'd previously constructed. He removed it, checked that the alarm wasn't going off before walking back into the trees at the front of the house. Dom surveyed down the street, making sure no one was about before hopping out and joined Carrie-Anne back in the car.

'How's the setup?' asked Carrie-Anne.

'The only thing that's going to stop anybody going in there are the portraits on the wall.' said Dom. 'I can't believe any woman would put those sorts of things up of herself in a house.'

'She was a former glamour model,' said Carrie-Anne, 'I mean, that was her business.'

'Well, that may be, but she knows nothing about security, a simple bypass to get in, but if they kicked the door and grabbed her, nobody's going to be here in time anyway.'

'Has she got any firearms? Anything to protect herself with?'

'One firearm, that's not looked after; it couldn't fire if she could even manage to load the bullets. I don't think she takes anything like this seriously.'

'The boss said so as well; she just rang me. She said we're on watch. She was also asking if we'd seen anything of her Russian friends.'

'Have you?' asked Dom.

'Incredibly quiet. Every other time we've been out, somebody's been after us. It seemed the perfect time to come if they were watching. You'd popped in there, we were split up; divided. The last time they came after you, when they thought you were on your own, they walked right into the trap.'

'Maybe they'll not be doing that again,' said Dom. 'Maybe they're looking for something else.'

'What is it then? Are you taking the first watch or me?' asked Carrie-Anne.

'We're not going anywhere. We do this together. Two pairs of eyes are better than one.'

'You're spooked,' said Carrie-Anne. 'You're actually spooked. I didn't think you could get spooked. Who is this Huntress?'

'It's a name. I've heard about it overseas. She's brutal, but she's also quick. I've had associates taken out by her before.

Not people that work for our service, people I knew over there, overseas when I worked around.'

'But who is she?'

'She's Russian and that is it,' said Dom. 'She's so good. Some of them didn't even know they'd been taken out by her. I found out afterwards. She's quite happy to let the name get out once the deed's done. We're actually ahead of her at the moment but know that she's coming.'

'You really fear her, don't you?' said Carrie-Anne

'I really fear what she can do but not to me. If she comes for me, she comes for the rest of you.'

'We can look after ourselves, Dom. I'm not just an analyst, you know. I have spent time out in the field.'

'So had my friends,' said Dom. 'Some of them were good, really good. I don't think Kirsten knows what she's doing going up against her like this.'

'It's the way Kirsten is with everything, Dom. It's who she is. She's a fighter. She's not a spy like you. She doesn't look at the long game. Kirsten's there to solve it, fix it, do it now. That's the way she is, in the midst of it.'

'Never understood why Anna Hunt took her on; she's not her type.'

'That's why she put you with her. That's why you're there. The teacher, the spycraft, they're a reminder of these things.'

'I don't like it, Carrie-Anne. I don't like it.' Dom moved his hand over and put it on Carrie-Anne's. 'I care too much about you, you know that.'

'Dom, I'm an analyst. Of course, I know that.'

Chapter 17

Anna Hunt stood at the end of the street in Aviemore dressed in black. She had trainers on, which was unusual for her, but tonight, she'd need to move fast. Tight-fitting light blue trousers and a black top allowed her to blend into the shadows. On her head, she had a black woollen hat, which when she rolled it down, would cover her face showing only two eyes. Around her waist was a holster holding a gun on either hip. It was very overt, but this was a simple mission. She was going to hunt and kill the one who'd been coming after her team. It had been a long while since she'd been an assassin, a long while since she'd gone out solely to kill, but times had changed. No one came after her team. No one would hunt and terrorize her people.

Earlier that day, she had hunted through Juliet's house. Godfrey had given up the address and Anna had gone through it with a fine-tooth comb. Hidden away underneath some floorboards was a wad of money. It was Anna's guess that the Huntress, having tapped Juliet, was getting her to meet at different times in different places. There was a high likelihood that the woman would be well protected for she was on foreign soil, but it was an opportunity that Anna could not afford to miss.

As she stepped into the street, a light rain began to fall and Anna allowed her jacket to fall down over her hips, covering her weapons. Her hair was tied up behind and she swallowed hard as she walked along the street, her eyes focused on the house towards the end. It was located in a terrace. There were no lights on in the other houses, but there was one single one in the target house, right at the top.

Slowly she walked along, scanning the entire street, seeing if anyone had picked her up. She doubted it, but she had to be thorough. She was also wary in case anyone else was about. She had to contain the damage all within the one house. She didn't want anyone coming nosing. It would take her a minute, maybe less, to get through the entire house. It had been a while and maybe she was rusty, but she doubted that. Unbeknown to everyone else in the service, she trained almost daily so that her firearms would be second to none. Both weapons were, of course, silenced, and by the time anyone noticed what was going on, she'd be long gone.

The jacket kept the rain off her shoulders, but Anna could feel her legs becoming slowly wet as the rain began to intensify. It was all good; it would muffle sound from outside the house. As she walked past it, she hurdled the low-level wall across the front of it. It was clever of them meeting in a terrace; they only had to cover the front and the back, but Anna would find a way in.

She crept down low, made her way up to the house, and sat underneath one of the windows. It was dark, but she knew somebody would be there looking out. There was always a guard on watch. Anna set her mobile phone up underneath the window, and with a small piece of tape, attached it to the underside of the windowsill. She had recorded something earlier and now set the playback in motion with the volume turned up full on the phone. As she did so, she crept over to the far side of the front of the house sitting underneath the other window.

'When we go in, you go right and you, left. We go in with the rear team coming in at the same time, are we all ready? Bravo is go; Delta is go.'

Anna could hear the playback from the other side and she hoped there'd be a reaction. 'Going in five, four, three.'

The front door opened, two men stepping out with weapons who then fired into the ground in front of the window. They never saw Anna as she dispatched them from behind, ignoring the tumbling bodies as she leapt inside the front door. Another man was there, but he couldn't react by the time Anna had already fired at him.

Bouncing left and right with her balaclava down, she saw an open door on the right and a figure inside. She dispatched him before turning and kicking the other door open. Someone was stuck in it and she stepped inside driving the man with the door, sending him spiralling into the wall. Someone leapt up off a sofa and Anna fired before focusing her other gun at the man who had been spinning.

Before he hit the floor, she was exiting the room, taking a shot at the person coming down the stairs. She saw him tumble but saw the muzzle of a machine gun coming in behind him and she spun to the cubbyhole underneath the stairs, hiding as bullets ripped up and down the hallway.

The door to the kitchen at the end of the hallway opened and Anna grabbed the person that came through by the hair, sending him spiralling along the hallway. The machine gun ripped down, taking him out before there was a cry of 'Stop' and, 'Oh, God, that's Vlad.'

Somebody spoke in Russian and Anna quickly peered out and back to see if anyone was there. The muzzle of the gun was still there, but nothing else. She stepped out quickly through the kitchen door to see no one was in the rear of the house but expected that someone might come through from the back if left unattended. Approaching the back door, she jammed a chair up against it before making her way back out to the hall. The house had gone eerily quiet, but things would happen soon for machine-gun fire had been heard. The police were probably being called in nearby houses.

Anna crouched down underneath the stairs, wondering what her next move should be. She'd wanted to do this quietly, and so far, she'd been smooth, but the machine-gun fire changed everything. She couldn't dilly-dally; she'd have to be quick.

Anna reached to her belt and the implements that sat at her rear. She pulled one out, checked the grenade she was holding, pulled a pin, and threw it up the stairs. There were loud cries in Russian before the explosion that would send ears ringing, but not Anna's because she'd covered hers as the weapon had detonated.

Long before the effects of it had subsided, Anna was leaping up the stairs. She slid across the top, guns aimed up and shot someone in the leg. Plaster board was strewn everywhere and a fine dust was in the air. As Anna went to get to her feet, someone emerged from the dust, grabbed her, and pinned her to the wall, hands around her throat. She saw the man reaching back with a knife, and dropping her gun, she grabbed the hand that was driving towards her, pushing it to one side and the knife tore into the plasterboard.

With one hand, she grabbed the man's wrist forcing it back off her throat before driving her head straight into his face. He bounced off the wall beside her and she drove a knee up into his stomach before pushing him to one side. There was a cry in Russian and Anna understood it as someone calling their mate to get down.

She flung herself to the floor, grabbing one of her guns before spinning over and firing into the mess beyond. There was a cry and she kept low as she came forward. The dust slowly settling, she saw a man on the floor and dispatched him before she turned the corner. Around her were three doors and she knew it would be luck to find the right one.

She kicked the one on her left open where a man stood with a gun and she barrelled into him, driving him back inside the bedroom. She rolled to one side as she heard a shot being fired and the man hanging over suddenly blurted out. As she regained where she was, she saw the man at the other end of the room who'd been hiding behind the door, and a quick shot took him out. After dispatching the man who was on top of her, she stood up facing the door and saw others coming and fired three quick shots off. They ducked out of the way, but she could see in her eye line someone in a distance, a face in a lit bedroom.

As Anna stared, something inside her was amazed. It couldn't be; surely, it couldn't be. She froze slightly as the image dawned on her; it was Control. It was Control's face. As Anna reached for a gun to aim it, automatic fire came into the room and she threw herself on the ground. She kicked the door closed as someone arrived, hitting him in the face. Quickly, she stood up and drove a wardrobe over on its side blocking the door. Gunfire came through the door and Anna remained down low; there was no way out of this now.

She couldn't go forward and see why Control was there. She'd lost her momentum. She'd chosen the wrong door to go through, and now the Huntress would escape, the mission was compromised. Anna looked behind her and saw the windows of the bedroom that would look out onto the front of the house. If she could get out there quickly ahead of them, it might just work.

She got to her feet, went over, and threw open the window. Beneath her was a fall of nearly eighteen feet, and if she just jumped, she'd probably break a leg on landing. However, Anna couldn't stay in the bedroom, she would need to move. Quickly, she leapt onto the window sill, swung herself out and looked up above her to see a drainpipe. Maybe it would do. She didn't have time to think.

She threw her arms up, grabbing hold of the drainpipe and started to pull herself up. She felt it shake and start to move away from the wall, and with her a free hand, she reached out and grabbed the bottom of a tile on the roof. She prayed it would hold as she swung her legs up and found herself half up on the roof, half down. The roof was slanted, and someone would surely come outside and start shooting at her. Anna just risked it and rolled herself as hard as she could up onto the roof.

Once there, she took her jacket off, throwing it down at the front of the house. If they came out, they'd follow her up that side of the street. Instead, she went up over the roof onto the far side, so she now looked into the back alley. Rather than descend, she ran along the rooftop trying to keep low. A tile slid out from under her feet and she crashed hard down into the roof and began to slide. She threw every limb out wide hoping to arrest her fall only stopping just before her feet went over the edge.

Quickly, she pulled herself back up, but continued along the rooftop, the rain still pelting down, making the surface slippery. As she got to the end, she grabbed hold of a piece of drainpipe and worked her way down to the bottom.

There were sirens screaming in the night. When Anna reached the garden of the end house, she quickly took her trousers off. She turned them inside out so they would show light blue. She did the same with the top and rolled up the balaclava, giving the appearance of a nice combo. She only had one gun left on her, having dropped the other one in the hallway and she put it underneath her hat and took her belt moving it round to the front. She unfolded the top over it so the other two hand weapons she had were covered over.

Emerging from the rear alley, Anna ran along as if she was out for a jog in the rain and saw two police cars passing by. One stopped, pulling over and an officer jumped out at her. Anna put her hands up.

'They came from that direction,' she said. 'Gunfire, did you hear? Gunfire came down that way?'

The officer thanked her, jumped back in the car, and turned. Anna watched it speed away into the night. She was passed by several more before she reached her car parked over a quarter of a mile away. Once inside, she drove out onto the A9 and back up towards Inverness. Eventually, she parked up and began hitting the steering wheel. She was there, the Huntress was there, and she couldn't do it. After a few moments of rage, she sat back in the seat looking at the rain falling down on the window screen.

Control was there, but Control was dead. They cremated Control.

Anna knew she was dead, how could she be there? Unless. Was it really this personal? Was this really revenge because of that? If it was true, then this wouldn't be over until one of the other side was dead. A chill ran up Anna, but she held onto the steering wheel, not allowing her body to shake. The Huntress would know that her security had been breached, that one of her contacts had been compromised. She'd be harder to find now, harder to spot.

Anna chastised herself before starting the car and driving off. She was still muttering to herself as she pulled up at the drive-through restaurant. She seethed, spinning out anger and swearing threats to the woman before she rolled down the window and was greeted by a happy teenager asking what meal she would want.

'Burger and chips,' said Anna happily, 'And I'll go large with that.'

Inside there was anger, but she knew what anger did. She would need to calm down and plan her next move, but she'd failed, and she hoped the team wouldn't pay the price for it.

Chapter 18

Dom was in a good mood. His charge was standing on the edge of the Moray Firth with an inflatable dolphin beside her. The sun was shining down on Kelly Haig and she was dressed in a bikini, although to Dom, the air was still fairly nippy. Maybe this was the unseen side of the glamour profession, having to stand and smile when really the conditions weren't perfect. It was a beautiful day, just one that probably required a light jumper rather than swimwear. Around Kelly was a cameraman, some boys holding lights and reflective boards, and a rather officious woman who seemed to be agitated that the shoot wasn't happening quick enough.

'Don't drool,' said Carrie-Anne in Dom's ear.

'My eyes are sweeping the shoreline, the sky, and everywhere else. I can barely see what's in front of me.'

'Liar.'

'It's a good spot, though, isn't it?' said Dom. 'We can see for some distance. It'll be hard to try and grab her here.'

'It would,' said Carrie-Anne, 'but on the other hand, this shoot's been in her calendar for a long time. Plenty of people know about it, so there's always the risk.'

'I can hear you both, you know that,' said Kirsten.

'He is actually drooling,' said Carrie-Anne. Kirsten could hear the thump as Dom obviously hit Carrie-Anne.

'Just keep your eyes peeled,' said Kirsten. 'The deadline's not very far away. If they're coming for her, they're going to come for her soon.'

'You never think about doing something like this?' said Dom.

'Like what?' said Kirsten.

'Standing in a bikini on the edge of the Moray Firth.'

'You're very glad you asked me that from a distance,' said Kirsten, 'because if you were closer, Carrie-Anne's thump would seem like nothing . . . and don't talk to your boss like that.'

Kirsten laughed inside. It was good that they were relaxed, for you worked at your best when you were calm. When people got tense, that was often when the mistakes were made.

Kirsten was sitting in a car a little back from the beach covering off the road that ran past the shoreline in case anyone would try to make a grab from there. She'd set Dom and Carrie-Anne up closer to protect Kelly Haig if anyone did get to her, but at the moment, everything looked good. Inside the car, it was warm, the sun beating down through the windows, the chill trapped outside.

Kirsten looked up the road, but there was nothing and her mind started to drift. She wondered how Craig was. Was he doing okay? Whereabouts were they hiding him? She wouldn't see him until this business was over, which was another reason why she wanted to get out there and face it. She was fed up with people coming up close to her. The pot shots, living on the edge wondering if someone was coming. She wouldn't have it anymore. She would end this.

'She seems to be having a bit of a row,' said Dom.

145

'What?' asked Kirsten.

'She's having a bit of a row. I don't know what the camera-man just asked of her, but she doesn't seem to like it. He seems to be explaining that actually, he's in charge. I'm not sure it's going that well for him.'

'Never mind that, what's going on around?' asked Kirsten.

'There's somebody paragliding out in the Firth. There's not that much wind, though. I can see some kayakers in the distance. There's a large boat, looks like some sort of cargo vessel chugging down the middle. There's a speed boat. Not along the shore at the moment. It looks like quite a nice one too. Nippy.'

'What's it doing?'

'Turning here, turning there. It's going wide from us.'

'Well, she's going back to stand and pose again,' said Carrie-Anne. 'It seems like the arty debate is over. Oh, hang on, she changed her bikini, that's what it is.'

'I thought the old one was fine,' said Dom. Kirsten could hear another thump in the man's arm.

'Oh, hang on,' said Dom. 'That speed boat, it's coming closer. Yes, it's definitely coming close to where we are. Maybe they're taking a look.'

'Full protocol,' said Kirsten. 'What do you see, Delta?'

'The vessel is coming closer, now beginning to pick up at speed. I don't know if he's actually making a run for the beach or whether he's just messing about. I have the binos on; I can only see one inside the vessel at the moment. An older man, his face looks very indistinct. A little bit unsure of what's going on with him.'

'Delta, Charlie, move closer.'

'Kilo, it doesn't look for real.'

'Delta, Charlie, move closer. That's an order.'

'Roger.'

Kirsten looked from the car down towards the beach and saw her two protectors get up from where they were sitting in the sand and move over towards Kelly Haig. The photographer stopped and turned to look at them, complaining about something.

Kirsten was out of the car and began running towards the beach. She could see the boat suddenly come close, turn sideways, and four men jumped out into the water. One pulled out a machine gun and started spraying bullets across the beach, but they were some distance away from Kelly Haig. Kirsten ran down to the beach looking for cover and saw Dom taking the photographer off his feet to ground.

'Delta, take him out. Take that man out.'

'Not much cover.'

There was a loud bang as the inflatable dolphin burst and Kirsten could hear Kelly Haig shrieking. Kirsten was still a good eighty yards away but went down on one knee drawing her weapon in front of her as one of the men ran from the boat for Kelly Haig. Kirsten fired twice taking the man off his feet. She saw Carrie-Anne begin to race for Kelly Haig, but the machine gun turned, and Carrie-Anne threw herself behind some small rocks. It wasn't great cover, but it seemed to be enough. As the machine gun sprayed towards Kirsten, she threw herself down on the ground hearing bullets pass over her head.

'Kilo, Charlie, they've got her. One of them has got her.'

Kirsten raised her head and saw Dom getting to his feet. The man with the machine gun was now trying to get in front of Kelly Haig, but was momentarily obscured by her. Dom used

147

the opportunity to run directly behind her, and as she was pulled to one side, he fired, hitting the man with the machine gun twice. Kirsten was up on her feet running hard towards the shore and saw Dom splashing into the water. He was close to the two men, both of whom attacked him. Kirsten saw him being pummelled back into the water. One of the men was then shot in the shoulder, presumably from Carrie-Anne and they turned, throwing Kelly Haig into the boat behind them. Kirsten kept running and the men kept their head down as they got into the boat due to the covering fire from Carrie-Anne.

'Charlie, Kilo, cease fire. I'm going for the boat. Get Delta out.'

Kirsten was aware that she hadn't seen Dom get up again, but her main focus was getting onto that boat. It was turning slowly, presumably, very close to being grounded. The men had kept their head down because of the fire from Carrie-Anne. The fight had gone quiet but they were cautiously peering back up. Kirsten made the boat as the engine started to turn faster. She made a grab, hanging onto the back of it as it started to pull away. There was a lurch, but she managed to roll up and put herself inside of it.

On the floor was Kelly Haig held down by the throat by one of the men, a gun held to her head. Kirsten ignored that for there was no way the man would shoot her. If they'd meant to kill her, they'd have done it by now. One of the other men went to raise his weapon toward Kirsten, but she put an arm out knocking the gun to one side, then kicked him in the stomach before grabbing him and throwing him into the water. The second man then came towards her, but she sidestepped in the small boat, drove an elbow into his back sending him sprawling, his head cracking into the engine at the back.

He tumbled to the floor, but Kirsten didn't have time to react as the man with the gun at Kelly Haig's head turned to put it towards her. She grabbed his wrist driving it up, but then saw the pilot of the boat turn to her as well. It was at this point that Kirsten realised the men were wearing masks, rubber ones, that made them look like they were old men. While holding the arm up of one man, Kirsten reached forward, grabbed the mask of the pilot, pulled it down so he could no longer see and had to desperately try and take it off his head. While he was doing this, Kirsten moved back to the man with the gun, bent his wrist backwards and she could hear a crack before she hit him hard in the knees with her feet. A couple more kicks to the stomach made him fall over. She reached down grabbing Kelly Haig by the hair.

By this time, the mask was off the pilot and he turned back for Kirsten only to find himself receiving a punch in the face. Kirsten hit him three times with a jab with her left hand putting him on his backside. She then reached down having pulled Kelly Haig to her feet, put one arm underneath her buttocks and threw herself backwards with Kelly off into the water. As she put an arm around the woman, she took her down beneath the water at first before she heard the comforting gunfire. She couldn't be sure it was coming from the shore, but Carrie-Anne would have had the wit, Dom too.

Thirty seconds later, Kirsten surfaced and saw the speedboat disappearing in the distance. She treaded a bit of water and started to swim back to shore, supporting Kelly Haig's head up on her shoulder and out of the water. The woman was snorting a bit, clearly having swallowed some of the sea, but at least she was alive. As they got into shallower ground, Kirsten felt some extra support, and Carrie-Anne put an arm underneath

Kelly Haig as well. Together, the two women carried the model ashore before setting her down on the sand. The photographer ran over asking if she was okay while Kirsten stood drawing in breath.

'Dom, is he?'

'He's okay. He swallowed a bit of water. Took a very bad punch to the face. He's a bit bloody, but he's okay.'

'Good,' said Kirsten and knelt down in the sand. 'That was a bit gung-ho,' she said. 'We got some, though, didn't we?'

'Yes, we did,' said Carrie-Anne, and then began to run off along the shore. Kirsten looked up and could see what the problem was. One of the men was swimming ashore, one she must have thrown off the boat. She watched him put his hands up as Carrie-Anne drew her weapon, but then the man reached down for a weapon of his own. There was too great a distance between them to tackle him hand-to-hand and she watched as Carrie-Anne took the man out with two clean shots to the head.

Kirsten looked around the scene. The police would be here soon, then would come all the questions and the tidy up, but at least with this one, the police knew what they were doing, knew they were here protecting Kelly Haig.

Kirsten looked down at the model who'd begun to sit up. A few minutes before, she had looked glamorous, standing, drawing the attention of men and possibly women, but now she just looked cold, almost a wretch. Kirsten watched her cough, and then she threw up in front of her.

'Has anybody called for an ambulance?' said Kirsten.

The photographer looked at her. 'The man's dead,' he said.

'No, for her and for me. She's been in the water, she'll get cold. Get us a coat or something.'

As she spoke, Kirsten could feel the chill herself. Yes, she looked impressive standing there, the hero rescuing the poor wraith in front of her, but something else was bothering Kirsten. Something was churning through her mind. She spun around looking all around her. Where was the second attack? If they were taking revenge, now would be the time. *Look at the state of me*, she thought. *Dom's practically down, Carrie-Anne's struggling to contain the situation. She's going to be busy. Where are they? They knew our other circumstances, and then suddenly they've vanished.* Kirsten's mind raced to Craig. Did they have something else with which to bargain?

Kirsten's mind was brought back to the present as Kelly Haig got onto her feet and threw up again. Kirsten surveyed the poor woman and the mess she'd become, but still, she was alive. Then Kirsten looked over at the body on the beach, the man who had the machine gun, who now lay dead. She glanced across at Carrie-Anne standing over the other dead man, and now they had a lead, people to follow. If they weren't coming to her, then Kirsten had to go on the offensive.

Chapter 19

After speaking with the police at the scene, the team made their way back to their Inverness headquarters where Justin was busy on his computer. They had sent three photographs of the dead men, and Justin had time to search and discover a few details. Kirsten sat in the conference room, a black coffee in front of her, Dom and Carrie-Anne opposite, while they awaited the arrival of their computer expert.

'You probably should get that looked at, Dom; there's definitely a cut across your cheek.'

'I'm fine, boss.'

'You can talk to him all you want,' said Carrie-Anne, 'but he won't do it. Not until we get somewhere with this. Where is Justin anyway? I thought he was ready to go.'

The door of the office burst open, and Justin marched in and stuck a dongle in a computer before flicking on a screen, and then sitting down at the table with a keyboard in front of him.

'Right, first things first: our five celebrities. I've done some further digging on the charity fundraiser that they were a part of for the orphan kids. I spoke to a Mr Michael Roy who made a complaint about them. Apparently, they all managed to take money out rather than add money to the account. They actually charged for their presence to be at this fundraiser. Basically, half the cost of the money that was raised at the fundraiser went to them, which seems a little bit cheeky if you asked me. There was a bit of a legal to-do about it, but they won in the end. Mr Michael Roy wasn't very happy, but I've checked him out and he's just the organiser of the event. I can't see anything on him, or any ties to any nefarious organisations.

'However, your two dead bodies are certainly tied in. Both are low-level activists: Alan Whatley and a Kyle McGovern. Funny enough, Kyle McGovern actually hails from England. Looks like he was up here out of the way. I've contacted some authorities down there to see what they can dig up. Alan Whatley, however, lives up in Inverness. I've got an address for you when you're ready to go. His name seems to crop up with a lot of close-to-the-bone groups, low-level, anti-celebrity heat, things like that. "The system doesn't work, we're all just getting used. All they're after is your money, promises, hits, TV, celebrity, lifestyle." Anything to do with that, Alan's been into it. We don't have any record of him using a firearm before, but certainly looks like someone who could be persuaded to get involved.'

'Good,' said Kirsten. 'Dom, Carrie-Anne, go check out the address, but be careful. If he's been compromised, other people may be on their way to help clean up his house, although I doubt they've been told very much.'

'If he's an amateur, he may be amateur about what he does,' said Dom. 'He could have left some clues around.'

'That's true,' said Justin. 'One thing about amateurs is they tend to write everything down; they can't keep everything in their heads. Either that or they stick it on the computer. If you find any laptops or that, bring them back to me,' said Justin.

Dom and Carrie-Anne nodded, stood up from the table, and had a look at the address that Justin had up on the screen.

'Do you want me to write that down for you?' said Justin.

'No,' said Dom. 'Professional here with a professional memory.' He turned on his heel and left the room.

'Take care of him,' Kirsten said to Carrie-Anne as she left behind him. 'We need to get a hold of Anna, find out where she's got with this. I'm just getting a bad feeling, Justin, I can't get a hold of Craig. I wasn't trying to contact him before, in case I exposed him, but we're not being hunted anymore. Nobody's coming after us,like they were before, which I don't understand.'

'You think they've got him? You think they're going to use him as bait for you?'

'Just seems weird, doesn't it? Why make all these efforts and then stop?'

'Maybe they realised you're on to them. Harder to do these things when you know someone's coming. Maybe so, are we getting teed up for something else? Are they making us drop our guard in not coming at certain times?

'They know though about these attacks,' said Kirsten, 'are you suggesting they're actually linked?'

'We've not got any evidence to say that.'

'No, but Alan Whatley is a low-level activist and he's now dead on a beach in Inverness from trying to commit a kidnapping. Some of the other kidnappings were much more professional. It's very blurred what's going on. Surely, if one was wholly professional, the next one would be. Why are there different teams? Why are there people involved here who just don't fit the profile?'

'I'll keep digging,' said Justin, 'but I don't know.'

'Me, neither,' said Kirsten, staring down into the black coffee standing in front of her.

* * *

Carrie-Anne pulled the car to one side a short distance from the address before stepping out and opening the boot of the car. She took out some extra weapons, storing them inside her jacket.

'You're coming in heavily packed,' said Dom.

'Seems like the occasion demands it. We don't know what we're running into at the moment.'

Together, the pair walked along the street towards the house before cutting into the side alley that ran behind it. From there, Dom gave Carrie-Anne a lift up so she could throw herself over the wall. She then opened the latch at the back, allowing Dom access to the rear yard. The house was a tenement and Carrie-Anne checked the windows around her to see if anyone was watching. When no one was, she gave Dom a nod and he made his way up to the door at the rear of the house, working for some two minutes before opening it successfully with his lock-pick tools.

Dom stepped inside, entering a small kitchen. He could see half-eaten food left at the sink and there was a distinct smell within the kitchen. It certainly hadn't been cleaned often. Carrie-Anne watched the rear door and windows while Dom searched the kitchen looking for anything that could give detail about what Alan Whatley had got himself into.

'For an amateur, he seems to have got himself into the big leagues. Where would he keep things?'

'I don't know,' said Carrie-Anne. 'Just keep searching; there might be something.'

The pair made their way into a small living room where there was a seat in front of a television. They picked up several magazines, all full of conspiracy theories. Dom noticed other magazines sitting beside a small sofa. He picked them up, flicking through them and realised he recognised the woman in them. They were from a few years ago, but Kelly Haig was certainly there and in some uncompromising positions.

'To think she gave this all up,' said Dom.

'Maybe that's why the guy was involved. Imagine it. If you're this sort of character,' said Carrie-Anne, 'you get a chance to kidnap Kelly Haig, I mean, they grabbed her in a bikini into a boat. The guy must have been bouncing to come and do this.'

'Indeed,' said Dom, 'but I'm not finding anything of substance.'

They went upstairs where there were two small bedrooms and a bathroom. On the back of the bathroom door was a large poster of Kelly Haig, but there was nothing untoward within the bathroom itself. A spare bedroom had a computer. Carrie-Anne pocketed the hard drive that was attached to it.

'Anything else?' she said.

'Not in here.' They made their way into the bedroom of the man and found sheets that smelled.

'He doesn't wash very much, does he, Carrie-Anne?'

'A single bloke on his own without his dream woman.'

'But why involve him? Why do it?' said Dom. 'The boss was right; the first time they kidnapped Angus Argyle, it was professionally done. Well done. Why involve somebody like this? Maybe they meant to get him killed. Maybe it's meant to throw us off the scent.'

'Why do this at all?' said Carrie-Anne. 'This guy. I mean, I get it, kidnapping Kelly Haig, but does he know they were going to execute her? He wouldn't want to see her executed. He'd rather bring her back here to the house, paraded around here wearing next to nothing, but he's not going to get rid of her because she's a celebrity. This is what the guy gets off over, isn't it? Her!'

Dom nodded, but he got down on his knees to look underneath the bed. 'Oh,' He said, 'look at this,' and he pulled out some boots that stunk.

'I don't think he goes under the bed, does he? Where else would you hide something now?' Carrie-Anne stepped forward, put her fingers underneath the mattress of the bed and lifted it up. There was a small notebook sitting on the base of the bed and Dom grabbed it before Carrie-Anne let the mattress drop again. He opened up the front page.

'This address is Kelly Haig's house,' said Dom. 'They clearly were after her. He's obviously part of the team brought in to do this, but why?'

Carrie-Anne made her way over to the window and looked down on the street. 'Dom, tidy up, we got to go.'

'What's up?'

'There's a car, it just pulled up outside. They're at the front door. Quick, under the bed.'

'Seriously?'

'Under the bed.'

Together, the pair of them pushed in close under the bed. Dom found Carrie-Anne lying in front of him. He put an arm around her, but with a gun in his hand so both their guns would face out.

'Quiet,' she said.

The door downstairs was opened, and they could hear a pair of feet making their way up the stairs. Several other feet were downstairs moving about. Things were suddenly turned over and the next two minutes was full of noise. Then the door of the bedroom opened.

Carrie-Anne could see a pair of feet, black boots making their way across the bedroom. The bed mattress was lifted up, the bedsheets torn off and thrown across the room. Then a hand came down underneath the bed. It grabbed the boot that was sitting in front of Carrie-Anne, then another. Then the hand came close to her face before they pulled a pair of underpants out from under the bed as well. Carrie-Anne felt she was going to choke with the smell that they were surrounded by, but her training kept her relaxed, ready to shoot if she had to.

Someone else entered the room and they could hear voices.

'Boss says time to torch the place. I'm getting the igniter now. Cover it.' A canister was placed down in front of them, and then Carrie-Anne heard somebody splashing fluid about. The feet remained until someone else came back into the room.

'Right, grab it and go.' Two of them remained there until Carrie-Anne saw a flame ignite and a large whoomph sound erupted as the room was suddenly ignited, orange flames burning brightly.

'We need to get out. Let's go,' said a man's voice. Carrie-Anne saw them leave the room. She rolled out where the carpet in front of her was on fire and managed to stand up just short of the flame as the room began to burn. Dom stood up behind her and together they exited the bedroom. The other bedroom was on fire. Dom looked out of the front window down to the street below.

'We need to go, Dom, out the rear,' said Carrie-Anne.

'I recognise that woman. There's an older woman down there. I recognise her.'

'It doesn't matter, Dom, we're about to get burnt. They're torching the bottom as well. Come on. There's a window in the bathroom here. We can go down the outside.'

'Where do I know her from?' queried Dom, but then a hand grabbed his shoulder and pulled him out of the bedroom onto the landing where the wall was beginning to ignite, smoke filling the area. Carrie-Anne dragged Dom into the bathroom before shutting the door behind and saw the large poster of Kelly Haig looking back at her.

In the bathroom, she thought. *Seriously? What does he do with that in the bathroom?* And then Carrie-Anne decided she just needed to leave. She threw open the bathroom window. Smoke was starting to come in underneath the door. Looking out left and right, she saw a drainpipe and swung her hand right onto it. Dom was following her, so Carrie-Anne quickly descended down to the ground. Dom followed and together they opened up the rear door of the yard looking out onto the alley at the rear.

There was no one there. They hadn't been spotted. Casually, they walked away and began to hear the cries of neighbours. Carrie-Anne hoped nobody would come near them because she was sure that the smoke was now embedded in their clothing.

Chapter 20

Anna Hunt watched from the shadow of a back alley as Dom and Carrie-Anne made their way quietly away from the now-burning house. She had followed them at a distance discreetly, making sure that no one was following them. When she'd arrived at the house, however, and the pair had gone inside, Anna had seen the arrival of another vehicle. Like Dom, she had seen the woman outside. The woman looked the spitting image of Control, but she was in the middle of the street and Anna couldn't risk a firefight, not with others around. So instead, once she'd seen that Carrie-Anne and Dom had got out safely, Anna had returned to her car and begun to follow the cars of the Huntress.

Three unmarked cars had driven off from in front of the house but soon had split up following different paths. Anna made sure she was following the one with the Huntress on board, keeping her distance, even as it had been a circuitous route around Inverness before finally working its way out to the A9 and heading south towards the Cairngorms. Anna wondered how far south they would travel. Once they got over Slochd Summit and settled into the drive, she reckoned they would soon reach Aviemore.

160

As she drove along, Anna thought to herself how strange it was that she had been operating in the dark behind the very team she was trying to protect. She hadn't been able to step out to Dom and Carrie-Anne, keeping herself to herself, operating solo when she'd advised that everyone else operate in tandem. However, Anna was not a young pup at this sort of thing.

Having gone at the Huntress already, she knew she'd have to be better this time, get in quick or else stay hidden, making a subtler approach. She'd know what to do when she found where the woman was going. The woman was a dead ringer for Control, though, and this was a family feud; it had to be, so the woman wouldn't stop, one way or another. Either Anna or the Huntress wasn't walking away from this one.

As she drove along the A9, several cars behind the one she was tailing, Anna thought how this life kept her alone. She thought about somebody like the Huntress coming for someone she loved, the hell that would be. She thought of Kirsten, how she got herself involved with Craig, and now she'd pay a price for that, be there worrying about him.

Anna did worry about her operatives, but it wasn't the same. They knew what they were getting into. While they weren't expendable, you did come around to the idea that you would lose some of them at some point. You never got too close. That was difference with a lover or a husband or even a child. Part of her wanted kids, but it never was an option with this lifestyle. They could compromise your mission. If somebody took them, if somebody threatened them, held a gun to them, your mission would go out the window. She'd seen mothers fight tooth and claw in a hopeless situation to protect their kids. With Anna's instincts, she thought she would be like that too. To be a consummate professional in this game, you needed no ties. The tie of her sister was hard enough, but then that was a tie she hadn't chosen.

Anna watched Aviemore pass her by on the left-hand side and wondered just how much further they had to go. A short distance after, the car she was following made a left turn and headed up into the Cairngorms. Anna held back further playing a cat and mouse game where she just about kept an eye on where the car was until it suddenly disappeared. She had passed two tracks, one left, one right, and she parked the car up and followed the one that had been a turn to the right. It ended in a holiday lodge with no one there, no cars, and so Anna made her way back to the road to look at the other one. The day was starting to fade, and she made her way just off the path that ended in a country lodge. The building must have contained at least six or seven rooms, and Anna hunkered down in the shadows out by some trees watching. The car she'd followed was there, as well as these other two, the ones who had turned off on different routes before coming here, but there was a fourth and a fifth car as well.

This must have been the base of operations, and as such, Anna didn't want to rush in. Last time, she went in quick and had come up short, making one wrong decision, entering the wrong bedroom at the top. This time, she'd find out where the Huntress was, and when she came in, she'd know she was in the room. Anna wouldn't hesitate with a shot, would put the woman down, clean up this mess.

Slowly darkness took over and soon the house became the only light around. Curtains had been drawn across windows but there was enough peeking through that Anna could see the front of the house up to the door. In the darkness, she made her way around completing an entire 360-degree view of the building, realising that there was a rear door for access as well, and one that didn't seem to get used very often. There was a barn off to the side but Anna saw no one come in or out of it.

As the hour approached midnight, Anna Hunt made her way to the rear door. She was dressed in black with her balaclava on again, ready, guns on her hips. Slowly she tried the handle of the door, and when it moved down, she opened the door just a peek. The kitchen area was in darkness, but she could make out a table in front of her, and she stepped inside, closing the door behind her before making for that table, positioning herself underneath it.

She heard footsteps, so stayed where she was as the lights came on in the kitchen. She watched a pair of shoes make their way over to the sink. A tap was run and she thought she heard a cup filling up. There were some gulps, the cup went down again, and soon the light went off in the kitchen. Anna breathed a sigh of relief and girded herself before moving out from underneath the table.

She reached the door that she thought would lead to either a hallway or possibly another room. Slowly, she turned the handle, opening it the smallest fraction she could. Inside she saw a man watching television. There was a set of stairs that led up, and the man had his back to the Anna. On one side she could see a gun sitting on a sofa.

Slowly she slid inside the door, closing it without a sound behind her. She stayed away from the man, keeping behind him, and moved silently across the room. She realised she was lit up now, a black figure stalking across, but maybe everyone else was asleep; accommodations would be upstairs. They were clever not posting guards outside. The last thing they wanted to do was to draw attention to themselves.

Anna moved to the stairs, stepping on the outside edge of them, a place where they were least likely to creak. She was nimble on her feet, more than many realised, and the years of ballet as a young child paid off now. As Anna reached the top of the stairs, the man downstairs stood up, and she heard him coming towards the stairs. She moved to the far corner, knelt down, hoping he couldn't see her from the angle he was at.

The man shouted something upstairs in Russian, and a voice from upstairs replied, but no one came out of the doors of the bedrooms. He turned, shrugging his shoulders, and made his way back to the seat in front of the TV. Anna was pinned in tight to the wall and down low and she waited for a few seconds before making her move. She stole quickly but quietly along the hallway but then turned a corner and she could see four different bedrooms. Maybe one was a bathroom.

She took the first door handle, turned it slowly, opened the door a fraction, and saw the room was in darkness. She slipped in, closing the door quietly behind her and crouched down, allowing her eyes to adjust to the lack of light. There was a bed on the far side, a number of boxes stored in the room as well. Quietly, Anna made her way across to the bed where a figure was lying, hands bound in front. She got up close, and almost gasped, realising it was Craig.

He'd gone into hiding. She hadn't even known where he'd gone. That was the whole point. Yet somehow the Huntress had found him, but she hadn't killed him; she'd brought him here. Why? Maybe it was a bait, the lure to bring Kirsten out of the shadows. Craig had been the one who had killed Control, but Kirsten was the one that exposed her. Kirsten was the one that had done the damage. The Huntress would want her. Killing off Craig would be losing a valuable piece of bait who could lure Kirsten out. After all, they'd photographed him with her, often at the same place.

Anna slowly undid the man's bonds. They were tight, and when he suddenly went to wake up, she slapped a hand across his face.

'Quiet, we need to get out.'

'Anna,' said Craig.

'The one and only, now come on. Are you able to move?'

'They've tied me up for the last two days. I'll do my best.'

'Here,' said Anna, handing a gun to Craig. Craig took it but was stepping in an awkward fashion across the room trying to shake out the lack of movement he had within his body over the last couple of days. Once on foot, she could smell urine off him. Had they not even let him go to the toilet at times?

She quietly opened the door again and her eyes fought against the light that was in the hallway.

'If you should go down the stairs, there's a guy in the living room. Take him out and head out. Get away as quick as you can.'

'You're not coming?'

'I'm going for her; I'm going to end this.'

'Then I'm with you,' said Craig.

'No, I work alone. You won't be a help. You'll be a hindrance, go.' Anna watched him start to go down the stairs, then made her way over to the next door, opening it quietly. She glided inside the room, shutting the door behind her, her eyes adjusting.

She saw somebody sleeping on a bed in the far corner. Slowly, she made her way over, looking, and realised it was a large man. He was snoring gently. She could finish him here, break his neck, but if he murmured, she'd lose the moment of finding the Huntress. That was the key bit. All the rest of these people, yes, she could take them out, but she needed the Huntress.

She made her way slowly back across the room, opening the door again, letting her eyes adjust before stepping outside into the light. She tried the third door. Once again, she snuck in quietly but almost fell over a table. As her eyes adjusted, she could see two people asleep. There was a duvet over them uptight and Anna stepped across quietly before placing her hand on the duvet and pulling it down, hoping to unmask the faces that were underneath. The first one was a male, tight black hair, and as the cover came off his face, he murmured, but lying into his back was hair she thought she recognised. It was long and wavy, and gently, she tilted the face back before looking at the image of who one could have thought as Control. Clearly, it was the Huntress.

Anna pulled out her gun, placed it on the temple of the woman. Once she pulled the trigger, she'd have to move. There'd be panic maybe, but even so, she'd still have to be quick as she could depending on how Craig had fared down below.

Nice to go in your sleep though, thought Anna. That was the way she would want to go if anyone ever picked her off. Without pain and without torture. So long. This will teach you for coming after mine.

Anna felt a hard thump in the back of the head and suddenly everything went black.

Chapter 21

'I'm telling you, I knew her.'

Dom climbed the stairs, Carrie-Anne following him up, and she watched him shake his head.

'You may know her from somewhere but maybe it's just a similar face.'

'No, I know her. We saw her before.'

'Where though, Dom? Within the service?'

'No. It's off a mission report. Somewhere, sometime. I need to get into the files.'

'You need to get into the shower first,' said Carrie-Anne. 'You stink. Go and get changed. You're not sitting around here smelling like that.'

Kirsten emerged from her office, as the pair rounded the stairs up onto the top floor. 'What happened?' asked Kirsten.

'We got in. We found an address, but it was Kelly Haig's,' said Dom. 'It was stowed between the mattress and the base of his bed. Then someone turned up, put fluid all over the place, and ignited it. We got out the back without being seen. Clearly, they'd come to sort his belongings out.'

'Dom says he saw someone there, though. He wants to check through the list.'

'Good idea. Probably best if you hit the shower though, first.'

'I did tell him that. Our clothes stink.'

Kirsten made her way through to speak to Justin, but the man shook his shoulders, indicating he had nothing further to tell her. Kirsten was getting edgy. She was on her own in the office, and she'd rather be out in the field, but it made sense. They needed to keep checking for clues, see the patterns in the kidnappings. Kelly Haig was still being processed by the police, and she was inside their station. The woman had been attacked, and she needed to make a statement and answer various other questions.

Kirsten didn't really want to bring her back to the office anyway, believing that the police station in Inverness would be safer, and so far, there had been no reports from the police about anyone untoward trying to interfere. If the botched beach landing was bad enough, there was no way they'd try and break into an entire police station.

Kirsten wandered back into the office, but saw Dom from a window, and walked back out to him.

'This person, what did she look like?'

'There was hair, blonde wavy hair, maybe tending towards a mousy brown, but it's the face I recognised. The angled nose, something about it. The hair didn't seem familiar. That's what I don't understand. I'll go take a look. There's plenty of stuff to read through.'

'Kelly Haig's all right, by the way. She's sending her regards up to us, apparently. You must be a bit disappointed, though,' said Kirsten, grinning.

'Why's that?' asked Dom.

'Well, I had to rescue the bikini-clad beauty. You probably wanted to do that yourself.'

Dom gave a grin. 'I'm too old for it, you know that. Either way, whoever rescued her, I didn't feel like doing anything coming off that beach.'

A pair of hands appeared on his shoulders, rubbing them. 'He's talking nonsense,' said Carrie-Anne. 'He'll be fine. Go on, go check those pictures. I need to get a shower of my own.'

Kirsten drew in a breath and got a whiff of what smelt like paraffin off Carrie-Anne.

'Yes, you do. Let's get on it, folks.'

Kirsten returned to her room where she sat with a cup of coffee, going back over previous reports of the kidnappings, desperate to see if she'd missed anything. She hadn't, of course, but it meant she was doing something. They drew a blank on the two dead men and with the house having gone up in flames, all they had was a single address that led back to where everything had started. Colin McGovern was clean. The police down south had found nothing. Kirsten paced around in her office; she needed for something to break. There was only a day left, one day, and then the next would be the execution of these celebrities.

Where were they? Where were they holding out? She needed to know. As was her custom, she wandered over to the window, looking down at the street. Everything had gone dark now. Night had come and her eyes wandered through the shadows, wondering if anybody was out there watching the building. She couldn't see anyone, but she knew better than to think she could see everything.

There came a rap at the door. 'Come in,' said Kirsten.

Dom opened the door and marched in. 'I got it,' he said, 'I've got it,' and wandered over to Kirsten's computer. 'Let me bring up the case files.' He tapped in some numbers and Kirsten sat down in her seat, watching the screen. 'That's one of yours, the recent one, the one where you shot the woman, Control.' An image came up on the screen of a dead woman. 'That face.'

'But she's bald,' said Kirsten.

'That was her, I tell you, spitting image.'

'She's dead; Control is dead.'

'Well, this woman wasn't dead out there and she had that face.'

Kirsten picked up the phone, and called the Service in Glasgow, requesting to be put through to the pathology department who carried out the autopsy.

'Hello,' said a voice.

'This is Kirsten Stewart.' She gave her authorisation code, causing the voice on the other end to become extremely officious.

'Yes, I remember. I remember that case. The woman was dead. She was cremated. I watched it myself.'

'You're sure the body burned?'

'She didn't walk out; it's an impossibility. We put it on, the flames went up, she burnt. Understand me, cremation is not a difficult thing. The people are dead, and you just burn them. They go inside the furnace. There was nothing left afterwards.'

'I'm just making sure.'

'Why do you ask?'

'We think we've seen this person.'

'Seen or seen someone like them? She could have a twin.'

She could have a twin, thought Kirsten. *You may be right.* She thanked the pathology expert, put the phone back down, and turned to Dom, 'Control is dead, Dom. That is not Control you saw. It may be a relative of Control, in which case Anna will need to know.'

'What does the Huntress look like?' asked Dom.

'We don't know. Nobody's ever seen her.'

'Yet, she's here, here because of what? For vengeance or revenge? You don't think?'

'I've seen stranger at the end of the day, why not? The family could be involved.'

'If that's the case then,' said Dom, 'we are in trouble. This is only ending one way or another. She might be talked out of it if this was business, but this is personal.'

'I realise that, Dom,' said Kirsten. *But I wonder, does Anna.* Kirsten picked up the phone again, dialled down Anna's number, but it was sent through to a different voice.

'Anna is currently undercover. I'm afraid that she's not available, Kirsten.'

'Do you know when she will be available?'

'She didn't say, she's gone dark, said she would contact when she was no longer dark.'

Kirsten thanked the woman, put the phone down, then stood up and made her way over to the window, looking down at the street. Her eyes didn't see anything because her mind was churning, thinking what was going on.

Anna must have known; that's why Anna's doing this; that's why she's going dark. Anna said she would sort out the situation, and for me to keep on the case. Maybe Anna was quicker onto this than me. Maybe Godfrey is involved.

'Dom, get that picture off to everyone again, make sure they're aware we could be looking for a relative of Control. Make sure they understand that this could be personal.'

'What I don't get,' said Dom, 'is why are we getting people like Alan Whatley involved? If this is the Huntress, surely the people would be professional.'

171

'No, they're dragging us out. They're making us come into the light, and then they're going to start confusing it with these amateurs. You're not going to want to take them out even if they have got guns. Or maybe they're a mix. Maybe Alan was the disposable one. That's why he was front and centre.'

Kirsten strode out of the office and in to see Justin, explaining to him that she now had a face for him to look for. 'Get onto the CCTVs, anything in the general area while in Inverness, where the attacks happened, see if we can pick up this woman. If we can, we might be able to pick up the vehicle, be able to pick up what she's doing, where she's moved to, find her location for her hideout, see their operations base.'

Justin smiled. 'I was just getting ready to turn in for the night.'

'Get on it. Give me what you have soon as you have it.'

Kirsten left the room, realising that Justin had only been making a little joke; he was good at that, keeping it cool and calm, but Kirsten was bothered now. *Why had Anna gone dark? Why didn't she have the team with her? The woman was formidable, but really?* Yet inside, Kirsten realised what she was really worried about. Craig. *Did he realise what he was up against? Was he secure? Was he safe? What had happened to him?* She sat down, her thumbs now twiddling. Hands then reached for the keyboard, and she typed in some nonsense before deleting what she'd written.

She got up, made her way over to the coffee, poured some, put it to her mouth, and then realised it was cold. She'd have to make more. She cleaned out the filter, put more in, set the machine on, then realised she hadn't filled it with water. Craig was affecting her. Craig kept coming to her mind. *Where was her London man? Was he safe?* She wanted to pick up the phone

172

just to know, wanted him to send her a text, but he'd gone dark. He'd gone quiet to make sure he couldn't be found. All it did was leave her with an unerring sense that he wasn't okay.

Kirsten made her way back to the desk, put her hands on it, and told herself that this was not helping. This was not allowing her to function. She needed something to do, somewhere to reach out to, but she was in the hands of Justin at the moment, seeing if he could come up with something. Every lead had gone cold.

No, she would need to act on further information. At least Kelly Haig was safe. The team had done that even though they were paying a bit of a price for it. *Why was this group wanting to kill celebrities though?* thought Kirsten. *But if the Huntress is involved and she's pulling us out, is this just a sideshow for me? A sideshow to get me out there?*

Kirsten looked at a photograph across the office taken of her in her police uniform. *They were simpler times, better times,* she thought. *Certainly, less complicated. You went after murderers. You weren't being hunted down yourself. Craig,* she thought, *where are you?*

Chapter 22

Kirsten heard the door click and immediately opened her eyes. Her sleep had been fitful as she was sleeping on the camp bed in one of the offices, but with the way circumstances were, she was already on edge. Kirsten turned and reached for the gun under her pillow, but the light flicked on, and she saw Carrie-Anne's face.

'Hey, don't shoot. It's just me. I've got the local inspector on the line looking for you. He said he's got news about Donald Hassim. Apparently, there's been an incident.'

Kirsten shot out of bed, dressed only in a pair of shorts and a light t-shirt. 'I'll take it at my desk,' she said, 'an incident doesn't sound good.'

'No, it doesn't,' said Carrie-Anne. 'I'll send it through.'

Kirsten stretched and made her way over to the seemingly permanently-on coffee, and she poured herself a black cup of it. She carried it rather bleary-eyed over to the desk and sat down just as the phone began to ring. She picked it up and announced in a pleasant tone, 'You're through to Kirsten. Who is this?'

'This is Inspector MacNeil,' said a voice on the other end. 'There's been an incident with our protectee. Donald Hassim was on his way from one safe house to another on the A9 when his car was driven off the road. I've got two police officers down, one in critical condition, but he's gone and we've no idea where. We're trying to locate the kidnappers, through CCTV, along the route to see if there's anything we can learn, but to be honest, it happened in the early hours of the morning. We did that for good reason, but we barely saw them coming up on us. Fast car, shot out our tyres, took out our escort at the same time.'

'Were you in unmarked cars as well?'

'Yes, we were.'

'Then I think there's a mole,' said Kirsten. 'We had one within our organisation as well. I suggest you start to look for it. Do you still have Kelly Haig in the building?'

'She's here, although she's getting a little uppity. Tried to explain to her about Donald Hassim, but you can't talk to the woman.'

'I'll be over directly,' said Kirsten. 'I think given the circumstances, we best take charge of her, take her to one of our places—they're much harder to find.'

'That's understood. She was your protectee after all. I'm not sure we're equipped for the amount of firepower coming at us.'

Kirsten put the phone down, stood up, and made her way over to a small wardrobe in her office. At first, she was going to put on a long skirt and a jacket knowing that Anna always liked the team to put on a good impression whenever they visited a place, but she didn't feel comfortable in such clothing. It was always more restrictive. She pulled on a pair of combat trousers and a tight crop top with a jumper over the top. She was used to fighting in this stuff. Kirsten needed to be able to take a swing with her leg or fire out a punch without feeling restricted in any way. Next, she fitted her holster, placed her gun in it, and put on her jacket before taking a walk out to Carrie-Anne.

Carrie-Anne was in the office she shared with Dom where the man was asleep in the far corner.

'I'm off out to the police station.'

'Alone? I'll come with you,' said Carrie-Anne.

'No, it's okay; it's only up around the corner. Besides, I don't think we're a target at the moment.'

'Really? You don't think they'd just take a pot shot?'

'No, I'm more worried about where Anna and Craig are. I'm worried they might have one of them and that's why the heat's come off us.'

'As long as you're sure. Stay on mic though, until you get there. That way I'll know you're safe at the station.'

'Good idea,' said Kirsten, taking her earpiece out from her jacket, placing it inside her ear and switching it on. 'Kilo check.'

'Charlie check,' said Carrie-Anne.

Kirsten gave a faint smile, but she could see the concern in Carrie-Anne's eyes. Still, she couldn't wait around all day, hiding away; she needed to get out and solve this and at the moment, Kelly Haig was in a precarious position. She was talking about leaving the police station, and she'd need somebody with her.

The drive to the police station was short and as Kirsten parked up at the rear of the station, she took a moment to scan the cars before getting out. As ever, her eyes glanced upward to that window where her previous office had been located when she was with Macleod, but then she walked through the double doors, stepped inside the main building, and made her way up to Inspector MacNeil's office.

As she approached, an officer came over to her, asking who she was. Kirsten produced a small ID and told him that she was expected. The officer knocked the door before opening it for her and Kirsten made her way inside. The inspector smiled and came over to shake Kirsten's hand but she saw on the sofa in the corner Kelly Haig, who looked angry. Maybe she was just annoyed. Kelly, however, looked immaculate.

The Inspector took Kirsten by the arm over to one side of the room.

'Hilarious, isn't it?' said the Inspector, 'look at her. She'd been shot at yesterday, kidnapped, pulled out of the sea and she comes and stays here. There's been a groomer come in, a seamstress. She's been dressed. I mean, look at her. Half of what she's wearing is hanging out there; can't have her parading around the station like that. We've got men here with work to do. Surprised they never took some hunk around so the women would be drooling as well.

'Frankly, Kirsten, she doesn't seem to understand her situation. I've been able to get her to stay until you arrived, but she was all for walking out. Four celebrities have been kidnapped. There was an attempt at kidnapping her and still, she doesn't seem to get the gravity of the situation. They said they're going to execute them. What's up with this woman?'

'Well, I'm no psychiatrist, but she's been up on a pedestal. I'm sure she's used to getting her own way whether that's through money or flashing whatever. I'll have a word. Besides, she's got to come back under my security. By the way, how are your people doing?'

'One officer is still critical. I heard you took a hit.'

'No, nothing much. Just a bloody nose. I hope your officer

recovers.'

Kirsten turned and took a good look at Kelly Haig and decided the Inspector was right. She looked like she was going clubbing and probably to a particularly hot nightspot given what she was wearing. Kirsten wasn't sure it was appropriate attire for the coolness in the air outside, but neither was she going to cramp someone's style. What bothered her more was that the woman wanted to walk out of this place without any protection.

'Miss Haig, I'm the woman who pulled you out of that speedboat yesterday.'

'Yes, you really wrecked my hair. That was when you picked me up.'

'Well, I assure you, it was done with utter necessity. The Inspector here tells me that you're thinking of leaving. I'm advising against that. You need a security detail with you. There is one day until the supposed public execution of celebrities that have been kidnapped. They tried to take you. They'll take you again. So far, we don't know where this is happening. It's not a case that if you get lifted, we'll be coming to rescue you. We can't guarantee that. I suggest you come into my custody, go under my protection for a couple of days until this all blows over.'

'Nonsense, I can't be doing that; got things to get onto. Can you imagine the publicity I'm getting off this at the moment? Need to tell my story.'

'You could tell your story from somewhere private.'

'No, I need to be seen to not be afraid. I need to be seen to be standing there. What do you think about this anyway? I thought this looked quite patriotic.'

Kirsten suddenly realised that the top which had so little

material in it, did actually have a St. Andrew's Cross on it to some degree.

'I'm not sure patriotism is what we need at the moment. Your safety is what's needed. You need to be coming with us.'

'Nonsense,' said Kelly, 'I'm not doing that, okay, so just go away.'

'I don't think you understand. I don't just go away. I've been charged with your protection; therefore, I don't go away. I might do it at a distance but I'm not going away.'

'You come near me, and I'll slap a suit on you. I told you I don't need protection now. I'm quite happy. I need to go out there and stand front and centre.'

'You nearly lost your life yesterday,' said Kirsten.

'What I got was the publicity dream of the year and if they take me again it's going to look even better.'

Kirsten turned and looked at the Inspector who simply shrugged his shoulders. Kirsten turned back. 'You realise one of my people was injured because of you? The Inspector's got someone on critical trying to defend your fellow celebrity. The least you can do is take this seriously.'

'I am taking it seriously. That's what you don't seem to understand. We're taking the fight to them right through the news media.'

'Miss Haig, I say again, you need protecting; get protection specialists if you won't take security from us.'

Kelly Haig stood up, then made her way over to the Inspector's phone, picked it up and announced proudly, 'Get me my secretary.' She then looked at the phone, annoyed.

'It's 9 for an outside line, then you'll need to dial in whatever number your secretary is,' said the Inspector. 'Feel free to use my office but please don't leave until we come back.' He then made his way over to Kirsten. 'I haven't had breakfast; come downstairs and have some with me, or I swear I'll kill her before she leaves the room.'

Kirsten smiled, gave a nod but turned back to Kelly Haig before she left. 'Organise your security and when it's there, I'll come and talk to you. When I'm happy you've got some, then you can leave.'

'You can't hold me here.'

'I held you up by the hair with one hand; that wasn't difficult. Holding you won't be a problem.'

'The Inspector won't let you.'

'The Inspector is going for breakfast. He seems a wise fellow.'

Kirsten watched Kelly Haig's face as she got angry before Kirsten left the room. After a quick breakfast with the Inspector, Kirsten returned up to the office to find that Kelly Haig had indeed organised herself some security. Two large men had arrived, both over six feet and when Kirsten came into the room, they looked down at her; their arms were huge. Kirsten wasn't impressed. Dom would look like nothing beside them, yet the man was quick, incisive, and could handle himself against the biggest louts.

Kirsten thought she could take the pair of them together, but they were at least a decoy, something there to ward off anyone else. 'Stay low,' Kirsten said to Kelly. 'If you're going to do an interview, go in an office somewhere, somewhere with plenty of people where you can lock the door, making it hard for you to be taken. Do you understand what I'm talking about, gents?' The two large men nodded back. 'Good, because she's under your protection now.'

'I don't want to see you anywhere near me.'

'In that case, tell me where you're going, Miss Haig.'

'Into the car, then off to the Thistle Hotel in the middle of town. I'm going up to the penthouse suite. I'm going to lock it off, and I'm going to stay there for two days. The only person getting in is someone coming to interview me.'

'Good,' said Kirsten, 'it sounds like you're starting to get the idea.' She turned and shook hands with the Inspector, again sending her best wishes to his stricken colleague.

Kirsten made her way back across Inverness, feeling the chilly air before she got into the car, once again thinking about the outfit Kelly Haig was wearing. What was it with some of these women? Certain times of the year meant she had to wear certain outfits, usually big jumpers. Kirsten stopped in the street outside her office, looked around, saw no one and then entered. When she reached the top floor, she could smell coffee coming out of her office and walked in to see Dom pouring himself a cup.

'I'm still working,' he said, 'it's just we ran out so I've nicked some of yours if that's all right?'

'Of course, it's all right.' She watched Dom make his way over and switch on the TV.

'Did it all go well with Kelly Haig then?' he said.

'She doesn't want our protection. She's going to go and lock herself away, top of the Thistle. She's got security guards all around, it's going to be hard to take her unless you're something professional. Even then, it's an awkward place to get to. I reckon they'll give up on her rather than go through with that.'

'Top of the Thistle, you say?'

'Why, Dom, what's up?'

'Look at that. What the hell is she wearing?'

Kirsten looked at the TV screen to see Kelly Haig standing in the middle of Inverness. She was wearing the same outfit she had been in the station, her hair not tied up now, but hanging down around her shoulders. At any other time, Kirsten would have felt slightly jealous that someone could make themselves look as alluring as that, but instead, she was looking on in horror.

'Dom, yourself and Carrie-Anne, get down there now.' Dom turned, put his cup down and left the room directly, while Kirsten made her way over to the phone. She picked it up and called Inspector MacNeil.

'What the hell?' he said, 'I told you, this is what she's like.'

'Have you got a number for her?'

'Only her manager, she wouldn't give her own personal number out.'

'Then give me that,' said Kirsten.

'Of course.' A minute later, Kirsten was ringing her manager, chuntering on the phone, waiting for him to pick up.

'Yeah, it's Alex.'

'Alex, this is Kirsten Stewart. Yesterday I pulled your client out of a speedboat by the hair when she was about to be kidnapped. She's now standing on an Inverness street corner after telling me she was going to the Thistle Hotel.'

'That was the idea, to go to the Thistle Hotel but we got invited to an interview by the BBC News editorial staff in Glasgow. 'Out front and centre,' they said. It's great, isn't it? She's doing well.'

'She's completely in the open. I've got people running there now. Where's her men as well?'

'Oh, they'll be off-camera.'

Kirsten looked up at the TV, and she could hear screams coming from it. As she watched, a car pulled up and two men got out, grabbing Kelly Haig and hauling her inside the car. It then sped off. She watched Dom and Carrie-Anne in the distance running hard to try and catch up. Kirsten put a call into BBC Glasgow asking for the editorial staff. She got put through to a man named Alan.

'Alan, when you made that call to Kelly Haig, who put you up to it?'

'Who put me up to it? I didn't make a call to Kelly Haig. Her manager called. Well, his secretary called, said she was about to make a statement so I sent the team in to film her.'

'Had you spoken to the secretary before?'

'Never,' said Alan, 'but that's not unusual. People turn over staff all the time. Why? Is something wrong?'

'Call your staff,' said Kirsten, 'Kelly's gone.'

Chapter 23

Kirsten had spent the afternoon in the heart of Inverness, looking for clues that would show where Kelly Haig had been taken to. She had seen Dom and Carrie-Anne arrive just after the abduction on her TV in the office. By the time she'd reached Inverness town centre, the circus had already begun. The police were doing an admirable job but in truth, there was so little to go on. CCTV was being checked, but the van was already burnt out on the edge of Inverness, and whoever had been in it had been switched to some other vehicle as yet unknown. Kirsten felt a little forlorn and while standing there, she felt the chill in the air. Tomorrow was the execution deadline. Would that be in the morning? How would it be done?

Kirsten was back in the office that evening searching through the CCTV reports, trying to work out where the van had come from. Dom and Carrie-Anne were back at base too, but the air was filled with frustration. Once again, Kirsten had the idea that there was a powerful hand behind this. At times, people who fitted the bill as a sort of activist were being used, but things were too clean, too easily swept up. No clue as to where to go.

She tried to call Anna throughout the day, as well as Craig. Kirsten had no success, and this was frustrating her as well. She needed her boss to discuss things with, to get a line on what was happening. She also wanted to know how well Anna got on with eliminating the threat hanging over the team. Did she have information that could substantiate Kirsten's theory, that the two things were connected? She wouldn't know until she got hold of Anna, and despite drinking numerous cups of coffee, Kirsten found it hard to remain calm.

She wanted a sounding board to go to, someone like her old boss Macleod. Someone you could chew the fat with and come out knowing your own mind on the other side. That's what she lacked now that she was in command. Anna should have been that person to talk to but she was never there. The service worked very differently to the way the police had.

It was one in the morning when Kirsten retired for a quick sleep, knowing she needed to be ready to move if something happened in the morning. The execution of the celebrities was hanging over her head but there was no evidence to follow, nowhere to be. She'd have to react fast when it happened. Justin Chivers was manning the night shift because he was the one person who wouldn't be going out in the morning.

Kristen was surprised when there was a knock at the door and her office was flooded with light. Her eyes blinked as she lay on the camp bed and saw Justin's face grinning at her.

'It may be time to make a move,' he said. 'I've just had Anna's staff on to me. She had gone dark from them, but she had the personal tracker on. Apparently, it's pinging but she hasn't called in to confirm it or deny it, so it looks like it could be for real.

'Where is it though?' asked Kirsten.

'Appears to be on the move. It started off down in the Cairngorms, but it's come out and it's heading up the A9 at the moment.'

'I take it we don't know what state she's in?'

'No,' said Justin. 'She might even be dead, but she did activate it. Quite recently as well.'

Kirsten rolled off the camp bed, stood up, and looked over at Justin. 'How are you feeling?'

'Fine. Why?'

'You look fresh enough. Suit up. Get the other two up as well. We're moving out.'

'You want me?'

'Anna is in trouble, she's not calling back. I need to take everyone I can with me. Besides, if my hunch is right, we may be getting led towards where our celebrities are, but just in case not, put a divert on all calls into here. Get Anna's staff to answer them. They can contact us if anything important has come through.'

'Will do, boss,' said Justin, leaving the room.

Kirsten stood in the shorts and loose t-shirt she had gone to bed in. She made her way over to her wardrobe, unceremoniously stripped off and then dressed in black attire. She checked her weapons before putting on her jacket and heard the knock from the door. Dom stuck his head in and then entered fully. Kirsten could see he was dressed ready to go and he seemed to be rather grim-faced.

'If Anna has pressed the button, it's all gone wrong,' he said.

'Not necessarily, we may be just coming to her assistance.'

'That's what I like about you,' said Dom, 'you're always optimistic. Me, I'm the pessimist. I think we go in heavy-handed.'

'That's why Justin is coming as well.'

'Justin? You know he's not a field-op.'

'Justin is more than you know,' said Kirsten, looking at Dom. She zipped up her jacket. 'Get the keys; time to go.'

* * *

Anna Hunt shook her head as she came to, and felt the rope biting into her wrists behind her. As her eyes began to focus, she saw Godfrey across from her with his back up against the wall, hands tied behind and feet tied in front. There were four guards standing around and one of them was slapping Anna on her face.

'Good, you're awake. The Huntress wants you ready for her when she comes back. Wants to sort you out herself. Have a bit of fun once she's got the business taken care of. Yes, all your mates are here,' the man said. 'Said you were a feisty little number. Is that the case?'

The man reached forward with his hand and started pulling down the top that Anna was wearing. She stared at him as his hand disappeared down inside. All sorts of feelings of hate were running through her, disgusted at the man, but her training told her to bide her time. She would have him.

Most importantly at the moment, she was under a death sentence, and she would have to react before the Huntress came back from wherever she was. Her eyes glanced over at Godfrey who was looking the other way, not focusing on Anna's particular torment.

'A bit pert, you look like a decent filly,' said the man standing back up. 'What do you think, boys?' The man reached down and grabbed Anna by the shoulder turning her over. 'Look at

187

the backside on that,' he said, smacking her hard on it.

Anna's feet were tied, and she was struggling to think of how to get out of her current predicament. The man threw her back onto her bottom and once again ran his hands around her body.

'She didn't say I couldn't have my fun when she was away. I think I could have fun with you. I like them feisty. Do you know that? Bet you wouldn't even scream, would you? Not give me the pleasure of that. Bet you wouldn't. Must be biting at you. You're there all helpless.' With that he swept his arm around, caught Anna with the back of his hand. Her head spun to the side before she turned back, grimacing at him, giving no sign of weakness.

'Hey, boys, look at this one. Oh, yes. She's going to be fun.' Anna stared at him, keeping his attention on her while behind, she began to dislocate her wrist. She felt the pain but she didn't let any show on her face as gradually her right hand was worked out of her bonds. She kept her shoulders in the exact same position but allowed the wrist to readjust and then gently unravelled the bonds around her other wrist.

'The Huntress says that's your boss. This guy over here, the old one.'

Godfrey looked up at the man and spat in his direction.

'No point doing that, granddad,' said the man walking over and kicking Godfrey hard. 'As for this one, he didn't put up much of a fight.'

Anna saw Craig's bloodied face lying in a corner. She wasn't sure if he was alive or not. She didn't have time to think about that.

'I reckon it'll be three to four hours before the Huntress is back, at least. I'll maybe give all the boys a go. What do you say, love?'

The man was clearly not Russian and spoke with a distinct English accent. The other men didn't speak at all. Anna got a distinct feeling he was a mercenary, although how good a one, considering the actions he was taking at this time, was questionable.

The man reached down and grabbed Anna's shirt and pulled her up to her feet. She saw his surprise as her bonds fell off behind her, but she reached forward biting into the man's neck. He screamed aloud as her teeth ripped into his flesh. She then pushed him back, nutted him hard, following up by driving her shoulder into him and ramming him into one of the men behind him. As they fell backwards, Anna followed, lifting a knife out from the pouch in the man's leg.

She stopped, turned, threw it, catching one of the other guards, clean in the throat. The fourth was in shock but began to raise his gun, causing Anna to roll to the floor and then sweep her legs round, taking him out. The man dropped, hitting his shoulder on the floor causing his gun to drop. She placed her foot on it, as she sprang up and drop kicked him with both feet hard in the face before seeing the first man, coming back towards her. Quickly, she freed the bonds on her legs.

He was enraged, so Anna let him come to her and stepped to one side and drove an elbow into his back. She then grabbed his hair before putting her arms around his neck and snapping it as if it were nothing. She picked up the gun under her feet. It was silenced and turned and shot the three other men, right in front of Godfrey.

'I see I pay you the big bucks for something,' said Godfrey drily, as Anna came over to him. She reached down with a

189

recovered knife and slowly cut away his bonds.

'You don't pay me big bucks at all; in fact, I've been meaning to talk to you about that.'

'He doesn't look good.'

'No, he doesn't,' said Anna, running over to Craig. She knelt down, put her hand on his neck looking for a pulse, then her head down on his chest. She could hear him breathing, although it was long and slow. She turned around and handed Godfrey one of the guns. 'Stay here a second.' She picked up another one for herself and made her way out of the door of the room they were in.

Anna had no idea where she was, but she walked out into a hall and then, opening another door, found herself outside. It was pitch black and she could see little around her, but there were trees. There was the sound of birds, but it was early morning, the light barely beginning to invade the darkness. She took a sniff and got that fresh countryside air. Across from her, she could see a house with lights on, and she realised she was at the abode in the Cairngorms.

At the front of the house, a number of cars were being readied, but Anna stayed in the shadows, wondering how best to play this. She crept up closer and realised everyone seemed to be leaving, except for the now defeated watching guard. *She was leaving a watching guard for me and the rest of them. Her intention is to come back, finish me, and do who knows what with Godfrey.*

Anna turned quickly and returned back to where Godfrey had been held. 'Looks like they're clearing out,' she said and started to strip in front of him. 'Get the clothes off him,' said Anna, and Godfrey went to the smallest man, removing his clothing and handing it to Anna. She dressed quickly, with a

190

balaclava mask over her, 'I'm going to follow them,' she said, 'Get some help for Craig, I'll activate the tracker.'

'You're going on your own after them?' queried Godfrey. 'How are you going to manage that?'

'They're all going to be leaving in the cars. I'll be in one; don't worry.'

Anna made her way out of the small room and out into the morning air. The light was getting better now, and she watched the first couple of cars begin to disappear. The last one was about to go, and Anna waited until the penultimate one had just gone out of view. Then she raced up, opened the rear door, and placed two bullets in the head of the man sitting there. When the others turned, she dispatched them quickly before putting a gun to the head of the man in the driver's seat.

'Where're they going?' she asked.

'They're following the route; the route's on the dashboard.'

'Thank you,' said Anna. She stepped back out, opened the driver's door and pulled the man outside, before shooting him. There was no hesitation, no second thought about taking a life. She quickly pulled out the other bodies from inside the vehicle, throwing them down onto the driveway, before clambering inside. The windows were tinted which suited her to a tee. Placing the gun on the passenger seat, she started the car and looked at the instructions on the dashboard. She'd need her tracker.

Anna decided she'd have to follow the instructions perfectly; they may have a tracker on the vehicle to keep an eye. After all, these were probably mercenaries, at least half of them. The Huntress would leave nothing to chance, even if they were going to the same address by different routes. Anna didn't have her phone on her, so she couldn't call; instead, she reached up under her arm and pressed hard within her skin. The tracker would be going off; her staff would tell Kirsten. Hopefully, they'd come. Otherwise, Anna was going to have to sort this out on her own.

Chapter 24

The feed from Anna's tracker allowed Kirsten to tail a car on the A9. The black Land Rover had tinted windows and Kirsten stayed well back. She had no idea of Anna's condition inside. The tracker would be inside her body, and she somehow activated it, but was she tied up in the back? If Kirsten got too close and got spotted, they might find that Anna was returned to them quickly, albeit not breathing.

The vehicle took a circuitous route around Inverness, then drove into the city centre before driving back out again, and then heading north. Along the road to Muir of Ord, Kirsten saw the vehicle take a hard left up a track and she continued a short distance before pulling her own car off into a different driveway.

'Gear up, let's go,' said Kirsten. From out of her own vehicle, Dom, Carrie-Anne, and Justin all stepped out, dressed in black.

Dom held up his phone in front of her. 'She's up that way, it continues up that driveway.'

Kirsten looked and saw the terrain rising slightly. 'Come on.'

The four traipsed their way through a small wooded area,

bending under the branches, doing their best not to make any sounds from the debris that lay underneath them. Thankfully, there was a dampness to it, so while the leaves may have rustled, they didn't crunch that loudly, and there was more moss under their feet than anything else.

Eventually, they got to a large wooden fence and Dom reached down, pulling at one of the planks until it came loose. Then he pulled out several more and held them up allowing the team to make their way through. Kirsten gave the order for silence, and then they fanned out as they crept their way up through a small garden before they could see a lawn at the back of her house. Through her binoculars Kirsten could see that a platform had been constructed.

The platform was a simple stage, but there was a wooden structure running over the top of it, descending from which were five nooses. From Kirsten's slightly lower position, she was looking up into the hollow underneath the platform, but she could see the lines in the wood.

'Dom,' she whispered, 'they're actually going to hang them. That's a drop floor.'

She scanned with her binoculars to the right and saw another small platform with a camera set up. There was no one around it, and she wondered what was going to happen next. Slowly, five celebrities walked out of the house alone. Angus Argyle was at the front and marched himself to the first noose. The second one was approached by Kirstie Macintyre and the third by Orla Devlin. At each one, Donald Hassim, the media tycoon, attached a rope around their neck. Kelly Haig was struggling to make herself come forward, but Donald had her by the hand, and he put the noose around her.

Kirsten noticed that the other four celebrities had their

hands tied up behind their backs. Only Donald hadn't. He then made his way to the fifth noose and put it around his own neck. Kirsten was struggling to understand for he had a grin on his face.

They must have drugged him or hypnotized him, she thought. *He wouldn't seriously do this of his own free will. Maybe they held his child.* Kirsten could feel her heart beginning to pound. They didn't know where Anna was either and they hadn't seen the car that arrived.

Ideally, she would have liked to have skirted around the entire house, but these celebrities were front and centre in danger. In her heart she feared that this was a trap, that they activated Anna's tracker on purpose. Was the Huntress this good? Maybe they had cut out Anna's tracker and she now lay dead somewhere. The celebrities were out in the open and in rescuing them, the team would be wide open to being shot. The situation was not good.

'Kilo, if we go up there, we're as good as dead. You're going to have to have somebody covering fire from here,' said Dom

'Delta, easier said than done though. Are we going to be able to hit that noose? Cut the string? Either that or we've got to bring the structure down.'

'Kilo, it looks well built,' said Dom. 'This is crazy. What can we do? How are we going to get out there without exposing ourselves?'

Kirsten wondered if she was being watched. Then she heard a whirring sound. She looked up above her where she could see a drone with a camera focused down on her.

Hell, she thought. 'All stations, they know we're here. They know what we're doing.'

Then the floor beneath the celebrities gave way, each trap-door abruptly opening. Kirsten saw them fall, swinging on the ropes.

'All stations, shoot the ropes,' said Kirsten. 'Shoot the ropes!' The team began to fire but the ropes were swinging, with the celebrities on the end of them. There was gunfire coming towards their position, and Kirsten indicated the team to fan out further. As she rolled to the ground and then aimed her weapon up, Kirsten managed to nick the rope of Kelly Haig. She saw the woman fall through the gap on the platform into the mucky interior below.

'Kilo, we'll never hit them all,' said Dom. 'Not quickly enough.'

'Delta with me. Charlie, Juliet, covering fire.'

Kirsten ran forward out into the open and heard her team firing from behind her. 'Tango down,' came Justin's voice across the radio. Kirsten leaped up onto the stage taking a knife from out of her trousers. From behind her, she heard Dom cry and thought he fell off the platform.

'Juliet approaching, Delta down,' came Justin's voice.

Kirsten at this point had reached Donald Hassim, and with a quick cut of her knife, the man dropped through the platform hole into the muck below. Kirsten ran for the next one but gunfire forced her back and she nearly tipped down the hole Kelly Haig had been hanging over.

Then she had a thought, and Kirsten rolled back into the hole landing in the muck below where Kelly Haig was quivering. She slid through the muck. Kirsten then picked herself back up and ran over over to a hole above her. Jumping up, she grabbed the edge of the platform, hauling herself through.

'Kilo, duck!' shouted Justin, and instinctively Kirsten went as flat as she could despite the fact she was climbing out of the hole. She heard the gunshots and looking behind her, she saw Justin spin and then fall off the platform. Kirsten flicked her head back and saw a figure at the end of the platform.

It had Control's face, but with long hair. There was a grin, and a weapon in front of her, with which Kirsten saw her aim. She threw herself to one side as a shot rang out and heard the cry of Orla Devlin. Kirsten threw her knife at the woman, whom she presumed was the Huntress, but the woman was able to dodge it.

Kirsten put her head down, running towards the woman, knowing she had to protect the other celebrities, but the woman fired, hitting Kirsten in the stomach, causing her to fall to the ground.

'Kilo, hold on, Charlie arriving.' Kirsten heard shots, saw the Huntress move back slowly, and then the woman grinned. Kirsten, holding her own stomach, the pain starting to pour through her, turned over and saw Carrie-Anne was writhing on the ground well off from the platform.

The three celebrities swung, and the Huntress walked forward, casually brushing them out of the way. She stood with a gun aimed down at Kirsten's head.

'You killed my sister, my twin sister. Some things are unforgivable, and I will go back and kill your lover. I will go back and kill your Anna Hunt, your boss. I will take Godfrey and sell him over to Russia for a life of pain. I've killed your team, or at least we'll make sure they're dead before we leave. You don't come for my kind, you don't play around with us, you should have let her kill Godfrey and she would have been gone. I don't care about you; I didn't even know you until you killed her.'

Kirsten tried to reach down her trousers for a small gun that was sitting on her thigh, but the Huntress walked over and simply stood on her leg.

'Enough,' she said. She caught Kirsten with the back of her hand causing Kirsten to hit her head on the platform. Her head spun and her vision became slightly blurred, but the words from the woman were clear.

'The thing about you people is you want to make a stand, you actually came after these people. Worthless, totally worthless people, but still you come for them, right into my trap. I had hoped for a bit more of a fight from you, a bit more, for they said you were something, rising up, but I find you're just as weak as the rest of them.'

The Huntress put a foot on Kirsten's stomach, pushing down in the wound.

'You could bleed out, but I am merciful.'

Kirsten watched in horror as the gun was pointed at her head. She closed her eyes awaiting the inevitable shot, then her ears rung with the sound of a single gunshot, followed by a second one. Kirsten opened her eyes just in time to see the Huntress fall backwards. A figure in black ran across her view, swung her gun up and fired to her left before she disappeared off into the house. Kirsten clasped her stomach; she didn't feel good. A voice seemed to be distant to her.

'Hold on, boss, hold on.'

'Dom,' she said, the words struggling to come out, 'Are you, are you . . . '

'Okay, I'm okay. We need to get clear. We need to . . . '

There were multiple footsteps running across the platform now. Kirsten looked up, her eyes still blurry, to see a dark-haired woman shaking her head right after taking off what looked like a balaclava.

'How is she?'

'Not good,' said Dom, 'she's not good.'

'The area is clear,' said the woman and she knelt down beside Kirsten, taking her hand, 'Hold on. I said they don't come for my people. I said that, but don't die on me now.'

Chapter 25

There was a white ceiling above Kirsten Stewart as she opened her eyes. It was clean with the smell of disinfectant in the air. She tried to sit up, but struggled, and then realised that she had a drip attached to her arm. She must have been in some sort of hospital but there weren't normal nurses about. It took only a few moments before Kirsten disappeared back to sleep.

She woke up three more times, only briefly before fading back. The fourth time she woke up, a man's face was before her, but it was blurred, and it took a moment before her eyes cleared and she saw Dom smiling at her. His arm was in a sling as he stood beside her bed. His face was covered in scratches, but otherwise, he seemed quite cheerful.

'How are you doing, boss?' he said quietly.

'I don't know,' said Kirsten. 'I really don't know. They're obviously pumping me with something.'

'They've had to do a bit of work on you. To be honest, we weren't too sure for a while if you were going to make it. You lost quite a bit of blood, but it seems you're going to be okay. A bit of recovery though. I don't think you'll be seeing work for another three to four months at least.'

'You'll be off for a while as well then.' Kirsten nodded at the man's shoulder.

'I'll be off permanently. I didn't want to do it to you while you were unconscious on a table getting fixed up, but I'm out. That was too close.'

'What happened? Where . . . What happened?'

'The Huntress, she was there. Anna Hunt happened. Anna Hunt saved you, but I'll let her tell you everything. She'll be in shortly. She's just taking a call from Godfrey.'

'But what about . . . '

'Carrie-Anne? Her leg's broken in three places. Got hit trying to defend you. Came off the platform, messed up and probably won't walk properly again.'

'And Justin?' asked Kirsten. 'He was behind me. I saw him get hit.'

'Justin will be fine. The bullet went through, caused some damage but they patched him up okay.'

'What about the Huntress? Somebody shot her,' said Kirsten. 'I remember. Somebody shot her.'

'Like I said, Anna Hunt shot her, protecting you. I think she's dead. I saw them taking her away on a stretcher but she looked dead. You know these things; they don't tell you.'

Kirsten let her shoulders rest. She looked from side to side in the room.

'What do you mean you're retiring?'

'I'm done with it. I am done with it. They came for us this time. I'm lucky to get out, and damn lucky to still be here. I've given my time to this Service,' said Dom. 'Too much time. I want a life. I want some time to go and enjoy. There's been too much killing—too many secrets. Now is the right time to do it.'

'What will you do though?'

'I don't really much care—paint, maybe go see the world, but I'll tell you something. I'm taking somebody with me. Carrie-Anne is stepping down too; she'll not walk again, not properly; she'll always have the limp. I asked her an hour ago.'

'Asked her what?' said Kirsten, feeling that the world was just rushing at her and she wasn't able to think straight.

'I asked her to marry me,' said Dom.

'And she said yes?' said Kirsten.

'No, she said no. She told me she wasn't getting married, told me she was going to elope with me, just run away. That'll do me. Just mind before Anna comes in; be careful how far you chase things in this profession. I did well,' said Dom, 'I got out, I'm still alive. I'm intact. I've fallen for a woman within the Service and she's coming out too. We're the lucky ones. You keep working for the likes of Anna Hunt, you'll end up dead, too.'

'I feel dead, my stomach is on fire.'

'Well, they patched you up good. Anyway,' said Dom as the door behind him opened, 'here's Anna; she can fill you in on the details.'

Anna Hunt approached and gave Kirsten a smile. There was bruising around Anna's face, but she was clearly in a buoyant mood. 'Look at you,' said Anna, 'fighting fit again.'

'Fighting fit for nothing,' said Kirsten, 'Dom says I'm going to be at least three months out.'

'You're taking six,' said Anna, 'I want you back in better shape than before. Besides, I need to recruit some extra team members now somebody's decided to run away.'

'I think my retirement is well earned, actually.'

Anna Hunt turned round to Dom and put out a hand. 'It is

and congratulations. I thought Carrie-Anne was going to be a keeper in the service. You managed to persuade her to quit.'

'We're not all married to it,' said Dom.

'No, but you'll come back if we need you. I mean, if it's serious.'

Dom raised an eyebrow, 'Only if you find me.'

Kirsten went to laugh, but then realised it hurt too much, so stopped herself short. 'What happened then? It's kind of a blur.'

'Quite simply, you were hunted. Turns out the Huntress is the twin sister of Control. When Control was killed, she came after you and Craig, and she caught Craig when he went into hiding. She didn't kill him at that time for she wanted to bring you back to him. She wanted him to see your dead body before she finished him off. She saw him as the main culprit, for he killed her sister, but obviously, you, me, and the team were implicated. She wanted to tear the whole unit apart. To do so, she set up the celebrity kidnappings, using local activists as well as some mercenaries. That's why things were sketchy, but she had a group of good people covering everything up so you couldn't get near them.'

'Celebrities? I shot the cord of Kelly Haig. She fell. Donald Hassim, he tied them up.'

'Yes, hypnotised, brainwashed, whatever it was, they're going to have to deprogram him, but he actually led them out. That was to make sure you couldn't take pot shots at anyone beforehand. You would see them, you would react to it, and then they'd just start gunning you down, take out your team, which I'm glad to say they failed to do even if it did rip it apart, and then take your body back to Craig.

'What were you doing though?' asked Kirsten.

Anna sat on the edge of the bed and brushed her hair back. 'I was doing what every good agent does. I got a hold of Godfrey, told him to shake down the unit, because someone was getting intel about where you were and what was happening. We found her.'

'What happened to her?' asked Kirsten.

'Well, let's say she doesn't work for us anymore. Anyway, from what she said, I managed to follow a lead and I went to kill the Huntress, but she had too many people around her. I tailed her again, and this time when I went in, they got me. I found out they had grabbed Godfrey at this point. I woke up to find Craig and Godfrey, but they left several mercenaries in charge of us while they came to you to get you and the celebrities. I managed to overpower them, follow them.

'I set off my tracker because I knew you would come. I believe they were going to set everything up and then get you to come to them, but she saw you were on the move, so they went and set the celebrities up, tailed you, but I think if you hadn't have gone to the right place, they'd have made it so you would. She always had this grand exit staged, but fortunately, I was able to infiltrate, be there at the right time.'

'I'm damn glad you were,' said Kirsten.

'You were good with my sister; you all were; looked after her last time. I look after my own.'

Kirsten laid back, feeling a tiredness sweeping over her again. 'So, she came to get us?'

'That's why you got photographed initially, making sure they got your identities, who you were. But Godfrey is something else. After Control lost him, the Huntress wanted Godfrey to take back as the head of our Service, auction him off back there. She wasn't going to kill him, instead keep him. Much more prestige. Still, she won't be doing anything anymore.'

Kirsten flashed a look at Anna. 'Dom said she was still breathing when you left.'

'Well, I doubt she'll be doing that for long.'

'Why, what's going to happen to her?'

'That's up to Godfrey,' said Anna. 'I don't think he'll keep her alive, too much of a risk, but you rest up, you've got to get better, then you've got to do some interviewing.'

Kirsten laid back and she heard the door open, and then close. When she next opened her eyes, the room was empty. Her eyes remained open for all of five minutes before she drifted away again. Carrie-Anne and Dom were leaving. She'd need to reset—she'd need to do a lot of things.

The next time she opened her eyes she saw the bruised and banged-up face of a man she hadn't seen in over a week. He reached forward wrapping his arms around her, and she hugged Craig back. Her stomach cried out in pain; it was uncomfortable, but she didn't care. Kirsten hung on to him as tight as she could.

Epilogue

Anna Hunt was wrapped up in a large black coat with a scarf billowing out behind her. She'd never been to this airfield before, though it was only a grass strip, but as she looked out into the darkness, she saw a twin-engine aircraft approaching. The moon was prevalent and reflected off the sea. Some landing lights were quickly put out and the aircraft touched down. Beside her stood Godfrey, dressed in a large coat, fighting back the cold that was biting into Anna as well. Adjacent to him, under an armed escort, stood the Huntress. She wasn't in good shape, her wounds having been treated, but still prominent and Anna had enjoyed seeing her struggle to walk along when she had left the car.

It was hard not to take things personally when they came for you, when they came for your team, but now that the Huntress was captured, Anna had let it go. The anger and the hate towards the woman, things that if she'd have let remain bottled up, would've eaten at her for weeks to come, if not years.

Anna said nothing as the aeroplane landed. It slowed before taxiing over towards them and she watched the engines shut down. The door at the side was opened and small steps were dropped down. Godfrey made his way over towards the aircraft where a man emerged wearing a small military cap and Anna failed to recognise who exactly he was. Godfrey spoke with him for a moment. Anna tried to lip-read but noticed that the pair of them kept out of everyone's view.

Godfrey then turned round and marched his way back towards Anna, before taking the Huntress by the arm. Anna saw her wince and she swore Godfrey was deliberately putting a hand where a bullet had caught her. He strode forward with her, and Anna watched as a small man with round glasses emerged from the plane. He was nearly as small as Kirsten and Anna wondered exactly who he was.

Godfrey stood with the Huntress approximately three paces away from the small man in glasses who was now being unhandcuffed by the man in the military hat. There was a brief nod and the Huntress stepped forward three steps before the man in the glasses stepped towards Godfrey. There was little ceremony before they turned and walked back, Godfrey placing the man in the glasses into the custody of the armed guards beside him.

Anna watched them march away, leaving just her and Godfrey there. As the Huntress popped her head back out from the aircraft door, she gave a wave and a smile at Anna, taunting her, and Anna forced herself to not reach inside her coat and draw a weapon to shoot at the woman.

'I hope he's worth it.'

'What makes you think he isn't?' asked Godfrey.

'She's dangerous and she could come back again. She knows me now, as well as Kirsten, you too, all of us, we've slighted her. When we slighted her the first time, she came and she came in abundance. I'm not sure this is a wise move.'

'I'm not sure it's wise either,' said Godfrey, causing Anna to stare at him, 'but sometimes we must do what must be done. The man in the round glasses has a lot of information. They have extracted some of it from him, of that I'm sure, but not enough. Certain things have not gone into motion that could've. He's more than worth it.'

'Well, I'll take your word for it. It's a tall price for the rest of us to pay.'

'Indeed,' said Godfrey, 'very steep.'

Any further comment was drowned out as the propellers of the aircraft began to turn. Anna watched as the flaps on the wing and then the elevators moved this way and that, as the pilot went through his checklist. Slowly the aircraft taxied out to the makeshift lights on the runway, turned, sped up, and then departed off into the air.

'It's too high a price,' said Godfrey, 'for she will come back for you. She'll come back for Kirsten, Dom, and Carrie-Anne too, and they won't have the protection of the Service. Justin, my staff, Craig, everyone, that sort doesn't work on business. The Huntress made it personal, always personal. You're right, too high a price.' Anna watched as the plane suddenly exploded in the air and parts of it descended down towards the sea.

'Kirsten said you told her that you look after your people. You must tell her sometime, you learnt that from me.'

Read on to discover the Patrick Smythe series!

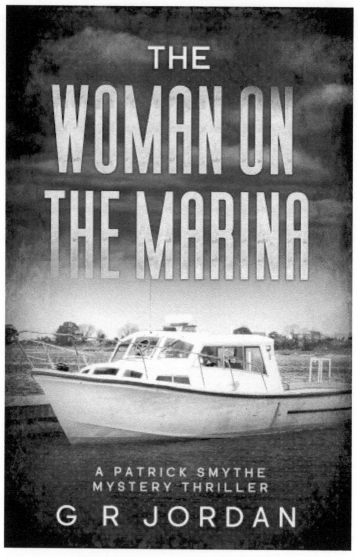

THE

WOMAN ON

THE MARINA

A PATRICK SMYTHE
MYSTERY THRILLER

G R JORDAN

Start your Patrick Smythe journey here!

Patrick Smythe is a former Northern Irish policeman who

after suffering an amputation after a bomb blast, takes to the sea between the west coast of Scotland and his homeland to ply his trade as a private investigator. Join Paddy as he tries to work to his own ethics while knowing how to bend the rules he once enforced. Working from his beloved motorboat 'Craigantlet', Paddy decides to rescue a drug mule in this short story from the pen of G R Jordan.

Join G R Jordan's monthly newsletter about forthcoming releases and special writings for his tribe of avid readers and then receive your free Patrick Smythe short story.

Go to https://bit.ly/PatrickSmythe for your Patrick Smythe journey to start!

About the Author

GR Jordan is a self-published author who finally decided at forty that in order to have an enjoyable lifestyle, his creative beast within would have to be unleashed. His books mirror that conflict in life where acts of decency contend with self-promotion, goodness stares in horror at evil, and kindness blindsides us when we at our worst. Corrupting our world with his parade of wondrous and horrific characters, he highlights everyday tensions with fresh eyes whilst taking his methodical, intelligent mainstays on a roller-coaster ride of dilemmas, all the while suffering the banter of their provocative sidekicks.

A graduate of Loughborough University where he masqueraded as a chemical engineer but ultimately played American football, Gary had worked at changing the shape of cereal flakes and pulled a pallet truck for a living. Watching vegetables freeze at -40'C was another career highlight and he was also one of the Scottish Highlands "blind" air traffic controllers.

These days he has graduated to answering a telephone to people in trouble before telephoning other people to sort it out.

Having flirted with most places in the UK, he is now based in the Isle of Lewis in Scotland where his free time is spent between raising a young family with his wife, writing, figuring out how to work a loom and caring for a small flock of chickens. Luckily, his writing is influenced by his varied work and life experience as the chickens have not been the poetical inspiration he had hoped for!

You can connect with me on:

🌐 https://grjordan.com

[f] https://facebook.com/carpetlessleprechaun

Subscribe to my newsletter:

✉ https://bit.ly/PatrickSmythe

Also by G R Jordan

G R Jordan writes across multiple genres including crime, dark and action adventure fantasy, feel good fantasy, mystery thriller and horror fantasy. Below is a selection of his work. Whilst all books are available across online stores, signed copies are available at his personal shop.

The Man Everyone Wanted (A Kirsten Stewart Thriller #6)
https://grjordan.com/product/the-man-everyone-wanted
A foreign agent goes rogue on Scottish soil. A city centre bloodbath shows the stakes at play. Can Kirsten secure the agent amidst a plethora of deadly friends and enemies?

When a shootout in the centre of Inverness ends in a mass of foreign bodies, Anna Hunt tasks recently recovered Kirsten Stewart with finding out why? When the trail leads to an agent who holds the key to a country's invasion, Kirsten must tread between friend and foe to bring the plans to light and stop a war. Will Kirsten prevail and avoid a myriad of friendly fire in the process?

You can always take a bullet for anyone's agenda!

Man Overboard! (Highlands & Islands Detective Book 19)
https://grjordan.com/product/man-overboard
A Coastguard's nightmare repeats. The fledgling tourist season is in tatters. Can Macleod and McGrath find the killer amongst the hordes of holidaymakers?

When the Coastguard note an increase in drownings from travellers falling overboard from passenger vessels, Macleod is called in to satisfy an itch that these may not be innocent accidents. When the victims are all found to be from troubled marriages, the team must seek the hidden orchestrator of spring mayhem. Can Seoras and Hope find the killer before widow maker of the seas strikes again?

To jump or not to jump, sometimes it's not a choice!

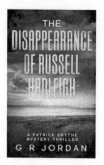

The Disappearance of Russell Hadleigh (Patrick Smythe Book 1)

https://grjordan.com/product/the-disappearance-of-russell-hadleigh

A retired judge fails to meet his golf partner. His wife calls for help while running a fantasy play ring. When Russians start co-opting into a fairly-traded clothing brand, can Paddy untangle the strands before the bodies start littering the golf course?

In his first full novel, Patrick Smythe, the single-armed former policeman, must infiltrate the golfing social scene to discover the fate of his client's husband. Assisted by a young starlet of the greens, Paddy tries to understand just who bears a grudge and who likes to play in the rough, culminating in a high stakes showdown where lives are hanging by the reaction of a moment. If you love pacey action, suspicious motives and devious characters, then Paddy Smythe operates amongst your kind of people.

Love is a matter of taste but money always demands more of its suitor.

Surface Tensions (Island Adventures Book 1)
https://grjordan.com/product/surface-tensions
Mermaids sighted near a Scottish island. A town exploding in anger and distrust. And Donald's got to get the sexiest fish in town, back in the water.

"Surface Tensions" is the first story in a series of Island adventures from the pen of G R Jordan. If you love comic moments, cosy adventures and light fantasy action, then you'll love these tales with a twist. Get the book that amazon readers said, "perfectly captures life in the Scottish Hebrides" and that explores "human nature at its best and worst".

Something's stirring the water!

Corpse Reviver (A Contessa Munroe Mystery #1)
https://grjordan.com/product/corspe-reviver

A widowed Contessa flees to the northern waters in search of adventure. An entrepreneur dies on an ice pack excursion. But when the victim starts moonlighting from his locked cabin, can the Contessa uncover the true mystery of his death?

Catriona Cullodena Munroe, widow of the late Count de Los Palermo, has fled the family home, avoiding the scramble for title and land. As she searches for the life she always wanted, the Contessa, in the company of the autistic and rejected Tiff, must solve the mystery of a man who just won't let his business go.

Corpse Reviver is the first murder mystery involving the formidable and sometimes downright rude lady of leisure and her straight talking niece. Bonded by blood, and thrown together by fate, join this pair of thrill seekers as they realise that flirting with danger brings a price to pay.